The Itinerant Way

PJ Kropp

Preface

It was in January 1988 when it all began. I had decided to adopt an itinerant lifestyle, via fruit-picking throughout the three eastern states of Australia. Over the next twenty years, I would persevere with this largely unconventional lifestyle: a lifestyle that would also take me beyond the Australian shores, from time to time.

This is the first book of a two-book series. I hope to have the second book finalised and ready for publishing by early-2021. In the early 1990s, I began to jot down handwritten notes as I constantly travelled within eastern Australia and abroad (Europe and New Zealand, in particular). Originally, I tackled both literary projects as autobiographical accounts. However, I soon realised that a different approach was required: a fictional-based one.

Although, most of the content of this book is largely fictional, *everything* is based on actual events and real people. Yes, I've let the imagination run wild at times, but the scope of the literary experience (or journey) would mostly be an enjoyable one.

Thank you for reading this page! Now – sit back – relax – and, hopefully, you'll enjoy my attempt at achieving literary prowess. Meanwhile, I'll be actively trying to promote this publication over the upcoming months and, additionally, will

be working steadily on the next several drafts (the first two
drafts have been completed) of the second book.

P.J. Kropp.

Contents

1

Enter the Itinerant World

During his time of confinement within the walls of the institution, Charlie Ash often contemplated the idea of entering into a lifestyle of *wanderlust.* Upon his 'release', Charlie immediately sought an affordably-priced motor vehicle. At a used-car yard, a 1971-model HQ Kingswood station wagon soon caught his eye. After parting with a wad of cash, Charlie (gleefully) drove the bulky but sturdy vehicle onto the busy street. With no power-steering and drum brakes (front and back), the heavy mass of steel soon earned a nickname: The Tank.

On a bleak and muggy day in early February, Charlie departed metropolitan Sydney for the upcoming grape harvest in the Riverina district (southwest New South Wales). The road trip to the city of Griffith (in the heart of the Riverina district), via the Hume Highway (M31) and the Burley Griffin Way (B94), would take about seven hours.

As he casually drove along the highway, Charlie's mode of thought was mostly one of positive aspiration – and hope. Would this new venture be the initial stepping stone to something much bigger: the genesis of an itinerant lifestyle, perhaps?

Upon arriving in the partially-dormant city of Griffith in the early afternoon, Charlie met his future employer in one of the local hotels. Constance 'Con' Cannelloni was an old school friend of one of Charlie's fellow 'institutionalised inmates'. The 'inmate' had provided him with Con's contact details, on a piece of paper. This piece of paper would largely provide the impetus for Charlie in his quest to start a new life outside a metropolis environment.

Still, in a state of road-trip weariness, Charlie's initial aspirations were soon dashed when Con coolly announced to him that the crop of grapes on his vineyard would not be ready for *several* days. Con, though, quickly informed Charlie that Luigi (his cousin) was seeking grape pickers for an immediate start.

A bonus for Charlie would be the availability of free accommodation, located in one of Con's vineyards. It soon became apparent, however, to Charlie that the antiquated and dilapidated hut had been unoccupied for a substantial period of time. As he wasn't prepared to dwell in squalor, Charlie quickly decided that he needed to undertake a sustained effort to make the humble abode more livable.

After a trip to the local supermarket, and armed with an array of cleaning products, Charlie commenced the arduous process of creating 'adequate habitation'. Communities of spiders (and other unidentifiable creatures) were swiftly dealt with, via instant extermination – courtesy of several cans of high-quality insect repellent. Then, he entered the bathroom.

The shower area instantly caught Charlie's eye. The ghastly sight of the odd-smelling, mouldy, fungus-growing shower curtain would have severely tested anyone's sense of sight and smell. But, alas, worse was to follow!

Reluctantly, Charlie moved the shower curtain to one side. The eye-ogling horror that lay before him defied sane belief. Hundreds of long-deceased bees covered the shower floor, with many more strategically strewn along the wooden window sill – and, even in the soap holder area. Eventually, all were removed, via the prolonged use of a dustpan and brush. After several hours and amidst fading daylight, an acceptable level of habitation cleanliness was achieved.

After devouring a prepared meal (heated in the stove's oven), along with a bottle of red wine, Charlie spent the remainder of the evening relaxing in an easy chair (or lounge chair). He slept well that night.

Early the next morning, Charlie awoke bleary-eyed and was greeted by bursts of unwelcome rays of bright sunshine piercing through the window – where there should have been a curtain. The unrepentant rays of sunshine mercilessly targeted his watery eyes.

Just after Charlie had consumed a substantial pan-fried breakfast, Con and Luigi were at the front door of the hut. Shortly afterwards, the three of them were on their way to Luigi's vineyard in Con's two-seated 'ute' (an Australian term for a tray back vehicle). Charlie sat in the rear open canopy part of the vehicle.

The vehicle passed through a section of Luigi's vineyard where bunches of grapes were hanging freely; easily seen, as they were barely covered by any foliage. A short time later, the trio was in another section of the vineyard, where the grapes were well concealed behind luscious amounts of foliage. The vehicle stopped here.

A pair of secateurs was soon placed in Charlie's hand. Then, Luigi gave a brief demonstration (which barely lasted a minute). Firstly, locate the grapes – well hidden within the luscious foliage. Next, cut the bunch of grapes and *gently* place them in a bucket. Each bucket was to be filled above water level, with a 'pyramid' of grapes placed on top.

Along the lengthy row, there were numerous empty buckets. Part of the row had partially been done. Charlie suspected that someone had quit the job recently – probably the previous day. Con and Luigi headed back to the vehicle and departed with the encouraging words: 'We'll be back in a couple of hours!'

Patiently and slowly, Charlie filled the empty buckets with bunches of grapes. After about two hours, he calculated what his hourly rate would equate to. Charlie quickly realised that this numerical figure was well below his level of desired earnings; aspirational motivation was fading rapidly.

As the day wore on with the temperature continually edging towards 40 degrees Celsius (104 degrees Fahrenheit), Charlie tried to convince himself that *things can only get better*. Several hours had passed; Con and Luigi were nowhere to be seen. His earlier level of patience had now transformed into a mood of mostly disdain and frustration. To combat this significant mood shift, Charlie decided to utilize an approach that involved an aggressive pruning technique. An eminent trail of mangled foliage, on the ground, soon followed.

Although Charlie was now filling the buckets at a quicker rate, his desired hourly rate was still less than adequate. As the end of the working day approached, Charlie decided that his first day of toil in Luigi's vineyard will also be his *last*. Absent for more than ten hours, Con and Luigi did finally return.

As Luigi alighted from his vehicle, his eyes were immediately fixated on the large amounts of foliage, roughly strewn along a lengthy section of the row. Sensing some kind of unsavoury showdown, Charlie's muscles soon tensed; he was ready for a verbal and a possible physical confrontation.

Still eyeing, unnervingly, at the trail of destruction, Luigi casually asked,

'So how did you go?'

'Bit of a struggle,' replied Charlie.

'It takes time.'

Luigi coolly added, 'Lots of foliage on the ground.'

'Easier to get to the grapes once the foliage is removed,' snapped Charlie.

Charlie enquired optimistically, 'When are you going to start on the section we passed by this morning … the neatly pruned section where the grapes can easily be seen?'

'Oh, that section isn't ready yet.'

Charlie suspected that Luigi was lying.

'Ok then, I would like to be paid my daily earnings … I need to buy food.'

Con then asked Charlie, 'Are you coming back on Sunday? We don't work on Saturdays.'

'Yes, of course … I'll be coming back!'

Charlie was taken back to the hut, but via a different route to the one that they had travelled on in the morning. He suspected that the neatly-pruned section of the vineyard was being reserved for *experienced* grape pickers. Charlie would soon learn that it was common practice that the better-maintained sections of orchards, vineyards or vegetable farms were often reserved for experienced itinerant fruit/vegetable pickers.

Novices, such as foreign backpackers or itinerant newbies, would often find themselves in the less-maintained sections of an orchard, a farm, a vineyard, etc. As most of this type of employment was paid by piece-rate, instead of an hourly or daily rate, this work practice would have a significant impact on one's potential daily earnings.

Back at the hut, Charlie was paid his day's earnings – in cash. After a refreshing shower, he drove to a nearby hotel where he enjoyed a hearty meal and several glasses of beer. The next morning, Charlie hastily hauled his meagre possessions into the vehicle and he was soon on the road again, driving southwards towards the town of Cobram (Victoria).

The road trip to Cobram took about two and a half hours. The serene, peaceful nature (but mainly dull and monotonous) of the trip would only be interrupted when Charlie attempted, on several occasions, to avoid groups of congregating galahs – inconveniently sprawling themselves across a sizeable section of the road.

Charlie quickly learnt that these grey-pink feathered creatures don't give up their positions on the road that easily! During the first encounter, *The Tank* 'collected' several of these stubborn feathered-fiends. Later, in Cobram, Charlie removed numerous feathers (and body parts) from the vehicle's radiator grill.

[Note: a 'galah' is also a derogatory Australian slang used to describe a person as a fool or an idiot.]

After the initial (and messy) encounter, Charlie resorted to the frequent use of the vehicle's horn as he approached any future road gatherings, in an attempt to minimize the carnage. The persistent sound of a blaring horn should have been sufficient enough to alert this somewhat imbecilic breed of a bird. They, however, were still reluctant to remove themselves voluntarily from the impending danger. This largely meant that the motorist needed to slow down considerably, especially when encountering a large flock of them.

As soon as Charlie arrived in Cobram, he immediately sought a café to satisfy his accrued hunger pangs. It was Saturday morning. The town was mainly in a comatose state; probably recovering from the previous night's alcohol-fuelled activities. Nearly all business premises were closed. However, a billboard with the words 'Big Breakfast' written on it, soon caught Charlie's eye.

Upon entering the café, Charlie immediately ordered the Big Breakfast meal: bacon, sausages, steak, mushrooms, baked beans, eggs, sliced tomato, and two pieces of toast (along with a mug of coffee). The large mug of coffee was soon placed in front of him but Charlie would have to wait a further twenty minutes for the gargantuan meal.

Whilst reading a newspaper, Charlie from time to time, would casually observe the only after patron in the café: an elderly gentleman (who had long, thick, grey hair and a matching grey beard) quietly sipping on his coffee – between reflective naps, with arms folded and head bowed.

After devouring the gargantuan meal, Charlie ordered another mug of coffee and continued reading the newspaper. Meanwhile, the elderly patron (with head bowed) began to snore – loudly. Charlie would extend his patronage to the café for a further hour, patiently waiting for a nearby hotel to open its doors at 11.00 am.

Just after 11.00 am, Charlie entered through the newly painted, swinging saloon-bar doors. Within several minutes, other patrons had arrived, including the elderly gentleman from the café. Sitting on a stool at the bar, with a jug of beer and a ten-ounce glass in front of him, Charlie soon found himself engaged in an earnest conversation with the barman and two of the early arrivals. The barman asked him whether he had obtained a fruit-picking position at one of the local orchards or not. Charlie replied that he had only arrived in Cobram several hours earlier.

The two local patrons sitting at the bar with Charlie were employed as permanent orchard hands on one of the major local orchards. Charlie was soon provided with a handwritten address of this orchard. Additionally, he was further informed that accommodation and *three square meals* were provided each day. The cost of the accommodation and meals, which were at a relatively low cost, would be deducted from an individual's weekly wage packet.

The pear-picking season on this particular orchard was set to start in two days. When Charlie finished drinking his jug of beer, he made his way to the orchard. By now, patronage at the hotel had increased significantly: a mixture of seasonal workers and local inhabitants.

Upon arriving at the office building of the orchard shortly afterward, Charlie soon found himself completing the obligatory paperwork: the *Employment Declaration* Form. The office secretary, upon seeing the name 'Charlie Ash' written at the top of the form, amusingly quipped, 'You have the ideal name if you are to be paid by cheque – 'Please Pay C.Ash' (please pay cash)!'

Twenty minutes later, Charlie was being directed to the living quarters. From the outside, the accommodation represented something quite bleak as the concrete walls were mostly of a murky grey colour with dominant tinges of dusty brown dirt (due to the lack of rainfall in previous months). The roofing was sheets of corrugated iron. Inside each room, *more* concrete: the floor. At the time, these cement 'doggy-boxes' were quite common on many orchards, especially the larger ones, within the Cobram/Shepparton region.

The furniture inside the humble abode included: a bed, which consisted of a well-used (and stained) mattress and an equally well-used (and stained) pillow; a set of drawers; and, a dust-covered wardrobe in a near-collapsible state. On the bed, there were two grey-coloured 'institution' blankets. This was to be Charlie's home-sweet-home for the next two weeks.

In the evening, Charlie would meet and greet some of his fellow itinerant workers, who were also residing in the cement 'doggy boxes'. Light-hearted discussions freely flowed, inspired by copious amounts of the 'amber fluid' (beer). Several of the older gents, however, were drinking fortified wine (either port or muscat) from coffee mugs!

Throughout the evening, it was quite apparent to Charlie that the majority of the itinerant collective was primarily interested in the cheap accommodation and the daily three-square meals that were provided! The concept of working hard and, subsequently, saving a vast sum of money, was of minor importance to them. The newbies/novices, in particular, were mainly in the orchard for the *experience.* Charlie soon learned that many of the itinerants had been previously institutionalized. In turn, they tended to regard the live-in orchard lifestyle as being similar to life on a prison farm.

The majority of the itinerants were either being paid the 'dole' (unemployment benefits) or the 'back injury' pension (the disability person). With the latter, the recipient is supposedly physically limited to certain lines of employment. Whilst an unemployment benefits form had to be completed and handed into *Centrelink* (a federal government agency) every two weeks, a disability pension form only had to be handed in once every *three months.*

Over the next two weeks, Charlie acquired a substantial amount of inside knowledge about the mindset of the average itinerant worker. He would learn that the serious itinerant workers would fill out extra *Employment Declaration* forms – a means to minimise their overall taxation payments. This, in turn, allowed these individuals to increase their level of savings during the harvest season.

Additionally, these experienced itinerant workers would generally have 'No Fixed Abode' as their residential address (stated on all *Employment Declaration* forms). A typical postal address would be 'Care of [insert town/city] Post Office.'

On Monday morning, and after a hearty breakfast, Charlie and the other aspirants had gathered in a section of the orchard where the trees were noticeably large and poorly-pruned, in readiness for the 'big' day ahead.

The group was soon introduced to the ganger (Jeff), who primarily managed and organised all the pear-picking activities on the orchard block. Jeff's first task was to allocate a block of six pear trees for each individual pear-picker. Heavy ten-rung steel ladders and well-used canvas fruit-picking bags were soon provided. Two empty wooden bins had already been placed on the ground, within each set of allocated pear trees.

Once all the pears had been removed from the allotted group of trees, the next course of action was for the pear-picker to gain the attention of Jeff, who would relocate that person to the next allocated block of six pear trees.

Initially, Jeff was ridiculously pedantic in his insistence that *every* piece of fruit had to be removed from each tree, before allocating the next set of six pear trees to be picked. Whilst some of the novice itinerant workers would climb a ladder to remove a missed pear, most individuals would just use the heavy ladder to belt recklessly against the branch and, thus, knock the missed pears to the ground.

Eventually, one of the veteran itinerant fruit-pickers, 'Rowdy' Ron (who was also one of the coffee-mug port drinkers) soon became embroiled in a heated row with Jeff. Ron, aged in his late fifties, soon became quite aggressive and forthright with Jeff and the following exchange took place.

'Hey, gangbanger, don't be so bloody stupid. This is a load of bullshit.'

Jeff sternly replied, 'But I'm only doing my job.'

Ron angrily responded, 'Bullshit. You get up the ladder and get the missed ones. I'll find my own next set of six trees to pick!'

By the late afternoon, Jeff had practically conceded defeat with this irksome, impractical work practice.

At noon, on each working day, the half-hour luncheon break would be taken. An assortment of sandwiches and fruit, accompanied by non-alcoholic beverages, would be brought out to the orchard block. Cool drinking water was supplied throughout the day.

Amusingly, some of the itinerant workers jokingly complained about not being allowed to consume alcoholic beverages (mainly cold beers) whilst they worked! At the time, the consumption of alcohol whilst working was a common practice, especially on the smaller-sized orchards/vegetable farms.

During the first five days, Charlie never departed from the confines of the orchard. On each of these days, the itinerant collective would be consistently entertained by the overzealous antics of 'Rowdy' Ron. Each morning, he would carry his 'ghetto blaster' (an oversized radio/cassette player) to the orchard.

Before a pear was even picked in the orchard block, Ron would have the oversized contraption blaring – loud enough for *everyone* to hear clearly – and painful for those suffering from a hangover. Just after the 9.00 am news, a well-known (at the time) radio talkback program would commence. Ron would then increase the volume several notches.

An overly-enthusiastic Ron would blurt out in a booming voice.

'God is on the air!'

'Listen up everyone … man with the golden microphone is on for the next hour. You might even learn something.'

Most of the group attempted to ignore Ron's belligerent antics, showing little or no interest in *God's words of wisdom.* However, an undeterred Ron would still regularly holler, 'Hear, hear!'

To further antagonise his fellow pear-pickers, Ron would occasionally clap thunderously and loudly declare: 'Sensational wondrous words of wisdom from God … the man with the golden microphone … hear, hear!'

After the 10.00 am local news, Ron switched off the radio and inserted a cassette tape into the audio cassette tape deck. For the rest of the day, anyone working within close proximity to him would be audibly tortured, forced to endure Ron's collection of *Country and Western* music. The orchard block, however, would soon be abuzz with a competitive array of other music genres.

Nevertheless and in a steely determination to remain antagonistic, Ron would occasionally start singing – loudly and awfully, mimicking the nasally-driven vocals of each song in his *Country and Western* music collection. His emphysemic gravel-sounding vocal cords were quite painful to listen to – particularly for anyone who was working close by.

During the luncheon break, on the Friday of the first week, the pear-pickers were informed that the following day would be a day of rest. Everyone had to finish picking their last bin of pears by 3.00 pm. After 4.00 pm, each individual could collect their weekly earnings from the office, located in the packing shed. The weekly earnings, paid in cash, were contained in an envelope. On the front of the envelope: the worker's name (often fictitious) was written; along with the number of bins picked for the week; their gross earnings; the amount of tax deducted; and, their net earnings.

Later that afternoon, Charlie (and other orchard residents), ventured into central Cobram and headed straight to the hotel, the same licensed premises he had patronised six days earlier. 'Happy Hour' had just commenced. Alcoholic beverages were at reduced prices for the next hour. Within a short space of time, *all* tables were covered with jugs of beer.

After Happy Hour had ceased and empty jugs had been removed from the tables, numerous platters of food were brought out. The food platters consisted of various pastry-based delights: party pies; sausage rolls; rolls filled with spinach and cheese; frankfurts embedded in layers of pastry; and, crumbed balls of mince and cheese. There was no need for anyone to purchase food that night!

Later in the evening, Charlie found himself sitting alone at a table with half a jug of beer in front of him. A short time later, a very large woman with a jug of beer in one hand and a box of chips (crisps) in the other, stood on the other side of the table.

Gazing unnervingly at Charlie, she attempted to initiate a conversation.

'My name's Shazza (Sharon)' and with a menacing grin, she added, 'You're cute … your name is?'

Next, she virtually shoved the box of chips in front of Charlie's face.

'Want some chips?'

'No!'

Sharon's dental hygiene was quite poor. On several occasions, Charlie had to face away – her halitosis (bad breath) was quite overwhelming. Sharon's face, arms, and legs were of a blotchy and reddish complexion. Even worse, her body odour was also quite intolerable and Charlie soon excused himself, stating that he needed to go to the toilet.

When Charlie returned, he discovered that his stool was now occupied by Sharon – her enormous posterior completely covered the top half of it. But, even worse, his half jug of beer was now empty. Provokingly, Sharon quipped, 'Hey cutie… you can sit on my lap if you want to!'

Charlie quickly turned around and went to the bar to order another beer. He then moved onto another table, joining some of his co-workers. An hour later, Charlie was engaged in an earnest conversation, when suddenly the light-hearted and amicable atmosphere within the hotel establishment was interrupted by an untimely and decibel-breaking commotion.

Sharon was screaming furiously at a scrawny wiry-built male who was a fraction of her size. Her hysterical tirade of words mostly began with the letter 'F' or 'C'. Then the volatile situation *really* escalated. Sharon began throwing punches at the hapless diminutive male. In self-defense (and desperation), he put up his arms to protect himself but one of Sharon's punches got through his guard and he collapsed to the ground.

Instantly, the publican, along with four other males, tackled Sharon and tried to physically force her out of the hotel. She refused to leave voluntarily and, on several occasions, tried to collapse to the floor. However, they managed to keep her on her feet. Eventually, the five of them managed to push Sharon through the saloon-bar doors and held her outside on the footpath. A short time later, she was arrested by police and taken away in a 'divvy van' (a police divisional van).

As closing time (11.00 pm) approached, the remaining hotel patrons were informed by the publican that a local police vehicle was parked a short distance away from the hotel. The local constabulary was hoping to nab any potential alcohol-affected drivers for DUI (drinking under the influence).

Many of the hotel patrons, including Charlie, were 'outer-towners' and had driven to the hotel. Most, if not all of them, were over the legal alcohol limit. 'Rowdy' Ron, however, had an ingenious plan! With a booming voice, he calmly announced that *Operation Decoy* was about to take place. Ron had already made arrangements with a teetotalling patron named Reggie.

Just before closing time, Reggie made his way through the saloon-bar doors and calmly 'staggered' towards his car, parked in front of the hotel. After dropping his keys twice, he then 'struggled' to open the driver's side door. After starting the vehicle, Reggie quickly drove away from the hotel and headed in a northerly direction. Predictably, the police vehicle gave chase!

Reggie took the first right turn. Although there were red and blue lights flashing behind him, he didn't stop until he was some distance down the street – well out of sight of the cars parked near the hotel. The remaining hotel patrons quickly got into their cars and quickly sped off, in a southward-bound direction.

Charlie stayed in the orchard for one more week. Realising that this venture was never going to be overly profitable, he decided to leave the area altogether. Charlie had already learnt from several of his co-workers that a large number of itinerant workers would make their way either to the town of Batlow or the city of Orange (both located in the state of New South Wales) for the apple-picking season, upon the conclusion of the pear-picking season. After spending two weeks in Sydney, Charlie decided to drive to the city of Orange. His itinerant lifestyle had well and truly become a reality!

2

Going Back to a Place in Time

After departing from metropolitan Sydney, Charlie drove along the Great Western Highway towards the inland city of Bathurst. After passing through Bathurst, he continued along the Mitchell Highway towards the city of Orange. Approximately ten kilometres east of Orange, Charlie came upon the idyllic town of Lucknow. A former gold mining town, it was the home of Australia's first gold-mining company: Wentworth Gold Field Company (founded in April 1852). The small town boomed throughout the 1860s and beyond until 1937 when all commercial mining there came to a halt.

The remains of the Wentworth Gold Mine are still clearly visible from the highway, especially the landmark poppet head (which still has part of the winding gear attached to it). Many structures, such as the miners' cottages, are still in existence. Charlie automatically felt a nostalgic sense of 'going back to a place in time'.

Upon espying the lone tavern (hotel) in the town, Charlie suddenly developed a thirsty quench for a cold beverage. After entering the premises, he promptly ordered a beer and sat on a stool in front of the bar. Also seated at the bar were two local patrons. They soon struck up a conversation with Charlie and introduced themselves as Jed and 'Spud' (and yes, his surname was Murphy).

Charlie's original intention was to drive to the west/southwest area of Orange, where the majority of the orchards were located. He soon learned, however, that these two gentlemen had been working on orchards in the Lucknow area for several decades and, hence, they were well aware of the localised labour requirements. An hour later, Jed rang a nearby orchard (owned by brothers, Kevin and Alan) and informed Charlie that employment was available to him. Accommodation for the orchard could also be provided.

During the initial conversation, Spud stated to Charlie that he could only physically work now and then. He further added that his 'working hours of capability' were divided amongst several of the local orchards. Jed soon interrupted. Smirking, he casually remarked that Spud spent *more* time in the tavern than he does in an orchard.

Undeterred by Jed's lack of empathy, Spud declared that he was currently receiving a disability pension; his physical mobility was limited due to chronic back ailments. Spud further added that he could only work a few hours on any particular workday, mostly in the morning. Again, Jed interrupted. 'Yes, he's back here, in the tavern – just after midday.'

Jed, aged in his late forties, was currently employed at one of the local orchards; he was picking stone fruits (nectarines, peaches, and plums) and pears. Jed informed Charlie that he will also be working on Kevin and Alan's orchard during the apple-picking season.

Several refreshing beers later, Charlie left the tavern and drove to the packing shed on Kevin and Alan's orchard, barely a kilometre away. He was immediately met by a friendly and pleasant-natured gentleman: Kevin (aged in his mid-60s). Charlie would not meet Kevin's brother, Alan, until the following day.

After a cordial but brief discussion, Charlie was directed to the living quarters, located inside the large packing shed. The packing shed also contained: modern fruit-sorting machinery; a very large cold storage room; numerous empty wooden bins; and, several tractors with bin-trailers attached to them.

The conditions of the living quarters were basic (but surprisingly very clean) and consisted of the following: several rooms, each containing a bed and set of drawers; a large barbeque, plus several gas-operated hotplates; a large refrigerator; and, a spacious amenities area. This was to be home for Charlie for the next three months.

Situated on one side of the packing shed was a large metal water tank, which contained captured rainwater: the only drinkable water in the orchard. This would be the first time that Charlie had drunk rainwater and he instantly acquired a likeness for this refreshing liquid. The rainwater's unique taste was quite *uplifting* and Charlie would refill his insulated five-litre water container at least once every day.

In the evening, Charlie put his barbequing skills to the test. After heating the barbeque, Charlie first added cooking margarine. As it melted, he spread it evenly over the hot plate. Next, a large piece of steak was unceremoniously dropped onto the plate. After a few minutes, sliced potatoes along with sliced onions and mushrooms were added. Sliced capsicums (peppers) were added later.

Later in the evening, Charlie decided to chill out in an antiquated rocking chair, slowly sipping on a 700ml bottle of brandy and reading a book containing a collection of trivia facts. Charlie slept well that night!

The next morning, Charlie woke up just after 5.30 am. A short time later, he was cooking his breakfast on the barbeque: bacon, sausages, eggs, sliced mushrooms, and sliced pieces of tomato. After consuming two mugs of black tea (to aid digestion), Charlie was ready for his first day of 'toil and hardship'.

For the first twelve days of the fruit-picking season, Charlie was paid a daily rate. The ten-hour working day

(7.00 am–5.00 pm) would solely involve the select-picking of several types of stone fruits: nectarines, plums, and peaches. The orchard block, containing all the stone-fruit trees, was about 500 metres from the packing shed. Transportation to the orchard block was provided by two drays, each attached to a Clydesdale horse. The two gigantic-sized horses were named Daisy (female) and Strawberry (male). Strawberry, however, was generally addressed with a more masculine-sounding name: Strawb.

Before departing from the packing shed, Charlie was first introduced to his co-workers: Alan (Kevin's brother), Rob (Kevin's son), 'Shorty' (whose real name was Sheila), Albert and Leith. The 500-metre journey to the orchard block would take about twenty minutes. However, Charlie enjoyed the slow pedestrian-paced journey. One could practically breathe in the serene and therapeutic feel of the orchard.

Alan, Shorty, Albert, and Leith would work from the dray being hauled along by Daisy. Kevin, Rob, and Charlie would work from the dray being hauled by Strawb. Each dray contained numerous plastic crates which would be later filled with selectively-picked fruit.

Once a certain number of these plastic crates were filled with fruit, they would then be loaded onto a truck (lorry): a 1930s Bedford model. This timeless, well-used vehicle had no doors, no windscreen, no engine cover and the battery was on the floor – next to the clutch.

On each occasion, it would take Kevin or Alan quite a while to start the truck – but these fellows were very patient. Eventually, the antiquated and heavily rusted vehicle would noisily roar into life. An accompanying large cloud of bluish-black smoke would emerge from underneath the truck as there was no exhaust pipe. The truck, however, would fulfil its purpose; successfully transporting the full crates of fruit back to the packing shed, several times a day.

Although Charlie found the fruit-picking process (only ripened fruit was selected) tedious at times, he was fortunate that he was working with Kevin and Rob. Both gentlemen were generally quite talkative and, thus, a variety of topics were discussed during the day. On the other dray – mostly silence. During the work breaks, Charlie would occasionally have a brief chat with Shorty, but he found it difficult to get too many words out of the other three!

Both Clydesdales were easy to manoeuvre around the fruit trees, due to their mostly placid nature. The pair were allowed to devour a piece of fruit now and then – they had even been trained to spit out the seeds. Kevin informed Charlie, however, that one had to keep a keen eye on Strawb. 'He could eat fruit all day long if allowed to do so!'

Over-consumption of fruit tended to play havoc with Strawb's digestive system. Occasionally, Strawb would lift his tail, drawing an immediate response from Kevin, 'Tails up!'

Kevin, Rob and Charlie would then quickly turn around and block their noses – the flatulent smell was ghastly unpleasant.

At noon, Strawb and Daisy would transport everyone back to the packing shed for the lunchtime interval. The lunchtime break would end up being about ninety minutes in duration: two twenty-minute trips and fifty minutes for the actual lunch break. Everyone sat on sturdy milk crates, in a shaded area, just outside the packing shed.

Nearby, Strawb and Daisy (after they had been released from the drays) were confined to a small yard, shaded by a large eucalyptus tree. There was mostly an eerie, but idyllic, silence during the luncheon break. Each individual was happily gorging on sandwiches or consuming a pot roast.

As Charlie was eating a sandwich, he noticed that Strawb appeared to be 'sweet-talking' Daisy. Whilst she was content to just stand patiently (and in a restive state), Strawb, on the other hand, appeared to be developing sexual tendencies towards her! The frisky Clydesdale tried to 'mount' Daisy, but she would discreetly shake her head and move slightly away from him.

Undeterred, Strawb would advance once again. After each attempt, Strawb's 'manhood' kept expanding: downwards. The well-known term 'hung like a Clydesdale' was being played out right before everyone's eyes – as they were eating their lunch. After several attempts to mount Daisy, Strawb finally conceded defeat. He seemed quite dejected. Poor Strawb!

After lunch, all and sundry returned to the orchard for the afternoon fruit-picking session. Sneaky Strawb still had to be constantly restrained from getting too close to the nectarines, although he still managed to consume quite a few – and yes, there were several 'tails up' moments. At precisely 5.00 pm, Clydesdales and workers were making their way back to the packing shed.

The next morning, before the commencement of work, Charlie decided to prepare a packed lunch: sandwiches, biscuits, and a thermos of hot black tea. He would stay in the orchard block during lunchtime which effectively meant a ninety-minute break. After consuming his meal, it was siesta time for Charlie. He would enjoy the therapeutic nature of being able to lie down and relax on the mattress-like grass in the moderately warm shade of a stone-fruit tree, breathing in the fresh rustic, orchard-odorous air, and listening to the sweet melodic chirping of petite-sized birds.

Some of these melodic sounds, however, appeared to be coming from the tops of some of the fruit trees. Some of these *little darlings* (parakeets, lorikeets, and starlings were the main culprits) seemed to be immune to the chemical sprays that were designed to prevent them from perforating (or pecking at) pieces of fruit. Whilst there were also several scarecrows in the orchard block, many of these tiny rascals were brazenly undeterred by their presence.

During the siesta time, Charlie would generally drift into a state of restive napping, only to be awakened or aroused by the 'alarm clock': the thudding clip-clop of Clydesdales' hooves returning to the orchard. Somewhat gingerly, he would rise to his feet. After some simple stretching exercises, Charlie was ready for the afternoon fruit picking session.

Although Charlie enjoyed this *modus operandi* approach to fruit picking, he was also eager to make some proper money (i.e. being paid by piece rate). Being paid by piece rate, generally, equated to a significant increase in one's earning capacity. After twelve days of working from the drays, the main stone fruit harvest (mostly peaches) commenced, where an individual fruit-picker was paid by the bin (a large wooden crate) rate.

Charlie was provided with a relatively new fruit picking bag: a (1&1/2 bushel) canvas one. The shoulder straps of the bag were uncannily similar to car seat belts. He was also given a grey Massey-Ferguson tractor, commonly referred to as a 'little grey Fergie'. The tractor was towing two bin trailers; each trailer carrying two large empty wooden bins.

The best-known 'Fergie' model, the Ferguson TE20, was manufactured from 1946 to 1956. In the ensuing years, Charlie would often find himself driving one of these little grey machines as many of the orchardists/farmers still had them. They were cheap to buy and the most common form of maintenance would either be a new battery or an existing one that required a recharge. The brakes on these tractors, however, could be best described as *suspect* – especially if one was towing a heavy load (e.g. full trailers/bins of fruit) down any sort of slope.

Unlike most tractors, which are diesel-driven, these grey Massey Fergusons are petrol-driven. Additionally, the gearbox only consisted of a single four-speed option. Other tractors had low and high range gear selections, which meant six or eight different gear options.

As Charlie had never driven a tractor before, Kevin soon provided Charlie with a crash course on how to drive one of these 'little grey Fergies' – with a specific focus on gear selection when going up and down slopes.

As sections of this orchard were quite hilly, Kevin stressed to Charlie that it was essential to undertake several vital steps before driving down a relatively steep slope:

1. Firstly, the tractor needs to be brought to a halt at the top of the hill, especially when the bins were full of fruit.
2. The throttle-handle needs to be at its lowest 'revs' (RPMs).
3. Select the second gear and let the tractor roll down the slope.
4. Do not touch the clutch or try to change gears as this will cause a sudden increase in speed.

5. Ignore the 'roaring' due to excessive RPMs of the
   engine and only attempt to change gears when the
   tractor is on a level surface.

At the time, the piece rate paid on Kevin and Alan's orchard was $20 per bin. On most of the other orchards throughout the district of Orange, the bin rate was $16-$18 per bin. Initially, Charlie was only picking four to six bins of stone fruit per day. However, during the short pear-picking season (eight days in duration) and the apple-picking season (two months duration), he was regularly picking six to eight bins of fruit per day.

As the orchard blocks of apple trees (and the block of pear trees) were quite a distance from the packing shed, bin trailers (each with two empty wooden bins) were brought to a nearby paddock. Therefore, Charlie and other fruit pickers only needed to unhook the full trailers of fruit (in this paddock) and then connect the empty bin trailers to the tractor.

By now, Spud was working in the packing shed and occasionally Kevin would get him to bring the empty bin trailers from the packing shed to the paddock. He would transport the trailers with full bins of fruits back to the shed.

On the second pear-picking day, Charlie was in the process of unhooking two full bin trailers when he espied Spud casually driving a tractor towards him. Spud stopped his tractor and gingerly alighted from it, only to discover that he had forgotten to hook empty bin trailers to the tractor! After a brief outburst of cursing and swearing, Spud quickly sped back to the packing shed on the tractor. Fortunately, for Charlie, there were already some empty bin trailers in the paddock.

Charlie later learned, via Kevin, that Spud had done this quite a few times over the years. Kevin further added that he had also been involved in other numerous *misadventures* during past fruit-picking seasons. On several occasions, Spud, in an alcohol-affected stupor, had climbed a ladder only to realise that he had placed it in a space – between two trees.

Spud's other great 'trick' was to keep climbing the ladder, forgetting where the top rung was. He would lose his balance and, subsequently, topple to the ground. Surprisingly, Spud never suffered any major injuries – other than a sore pride.

The apple-picking season commenced in mid-March. Four other seasonal fruit pickers were to join Charlie for this particular two-month season. Jed, Tommi (a Finnish-born itinerant), Bill, and Ben.

Charlie soon learnt that all four of them were veteran seasonal workers, having each been in the itinerant fruit-picking game for more than two decades. During this two-month season, these four gentlemen proved to be a *wealth of information* for Charlie. Collectively, they had worked and travelled throughout Australia and in many other countries: New Zealand, the USA, Canada, and various European countries.

In the local tavern and the living quarters of the packing shed, Charlie would regularly quiz them on their past travelling experiences. These frank and informative discussions were to provide Charlie with the impetus to adopt an itinerant lifestyle for, at least, the next few years. Although he did not know it at the time, Charlie's *wanderlust* of an itinerant, nomadic lifestyle would last for more than twenty years!

During April, there was a one-week break between the red varieties of apples and the Granny Smith apples. Charlie managed to fill in this one-week void by obtaining employment at another orchard (located a few kilometres south-west of the Orange) in an area roughly situated between Lake Canobolas and Mount Canobolas (an extinct volcano and 1395m above sea level). In this period of employment, Charlie would never meet the owner of the orchard, Rudolpho Clounifanni, but he would soon learn plenty about him!

The day-to-day operations were under the command of the orchard manager. Jim (aged in his 60s), on several occasions, would cheekily inform Charlie of some of Rudolpho's past misdemeanours. In the ensuing years, though, Charlie would learn even far more about Rudolpho –

especially from other orchardists – basically regarding him as an unscrupulous rogue.

The orchard wasn't anywhere near as well maintained as Kevin and Alan's orchard. Even worse, the bin rate was less. At the end of the week, Charlie was supposed to be paid by cheque. Jim explained to Charlie, however, that Rudolpho had endured an *unfortunate mishap* at the 'Flemo Markets' and, subsequently, had gone 'missing' or in other words – had placed himself in a self-imposed exile.

Rudolpho, allegedly, had been *scalped* by 'market mafioso' as a warning to a long-overdue unpaid debt. Word of his misfortune spread rapidly throughout the orcharding community! Charlie later learned that most of Rudolpho's hair had been removed – along with numerous scalpel marks on his bald head.

Fortunately, for Charlie and the other apple pickers, Jim arranged for them to be paid in cash at a fruit and vegetable store; owned by Rudolpho's elderly parents. For several future fruit-picking seasons, Charlie would often buy fruit and vegetables from this particular store.

Inside the fruit and vegetable store, there was a relatively-new cash register on the side of the counter bench. It was seldom used. The ageing Mrs. Clounifanni preferred to write down on a piece of paper (in pencil) a list of items and their corresponding prices purchased by the customer. It soon emerged, however, that her arithmetic skills appeared to be quite poor.

When totalling the cost of all the items, her calculations were often incorrect. To combat this problem, Charlie would bring a calculator with him. After the purchase was completed, Mrs. Clounifanni would put the notes and coins in a drawer – located below the cash register.

Although Charlie never met Rudolpho, his younger brother (Valentino) would occasionally put in a 'guest appearance' at the orchard. Valentino would only converse with Jim and blatantly ignored the presence of any nearby fruit pickers. Not even a simple hello!

Charlie, though, didn't care that he was snubbed by Valentino; he took an instant dislike to him anyway. His appearance said *everything*. Valentino was always immaculately dressed – as if he was about to go to a nightclub. Around his neck, he wore several gold chains, along with an expensive-looking designer shirt and expensive (and shiny) pointed shoes. To top it off, Valentino's thick black (and slicked-back) hair appeared to contain an excessive amount of oil!

On one of the working days, Charlie was working in a section of the orchard that was near a high-fenced secured forest-like area. There was plenty of 'Do Not Enter', 'No Trespassing', and 'Electric Fence' signs being displayed. At one point, Charlie was tempted to climb over the fence and explore this forest-like area. However, as the fence was supposedly electrified, he decided to remain in the orchard block.

A few months later, Charlie learnt that this secured area had been raided by police authorities. The confined area contained a *substantially-sized* marijuana plantation that had been under surveillance for quite a while. Rudolpho and Valentino, subsequently, were arrested and questioned. Both of them denied any knowledge of the plantation. The supposed surveillance never produced any photographic evidence of them ever being in this area! As a result, neither was charged with any illegal substance-cultivating offences.

After the week-long tenure at Clounifanni's orchard, Charlie returned to Kevin and Alan's orchard as the Granny Smith apple harvest was about to commence. It was the third week in April. Whilst the harvest would only last for three weeks, Charlie earned (and saved) quite a reasonable amount of money, despite several late-starting times due to 'dewy' mornings. Whilst the apples were still wet, Kevin would stress (to the itinerant workers) that they needed to be 'gentler' as the skins of the Granny Smith apples tended to bruise more easily when covered in dew – especially finger bruising.

In the second week of May, the fruit picking season at Kevin and Alan's came to a halt. Most of the apple-picking season in the Orange region was now complete. However, courtesy of a casual conversation with Jed in the tavern, Charlie learnt of another orchard (about five kilometres away) that required apple-pickers for nearly two weeks' worth of employment. As winter was fast approaching, along with substantially reduced temperatures, the vast majority of itinerant seasonal workers had already left the area. Many of them had relocated to 'sunny' Queensland.

Charlie would complete this apple-picking season at Comeforth Orchard, owned by an elderly couple: Ernie and Daphne Breezer. The mornings were consistently cold and damp, due to the heavy dews. Fortunately, the afternoon weather conditions were generally much more favourable.

As the orchard consisted of several hilly areas, Charlie was soon presented with opportunities to further develop his tractor-driving skills. He quickly discovered that it was impossible to stop on any downward slopes in the morning; the wet lush grass (from the heavy dew) ensured this scenario. When bringing full bins of fruit back to the packing shed, Charlie had to negotiate a steep and rocky decline, just before reaching a levelled cemented area in front of the packing shed.

During this period of employment, Charlie generally worked between 9.00 am and 5.00 pm. Every morning, his work boots and the lower part of his trousers would be soaked from the semi-long, dewy grass – a discomfort that he would have to endure for at least several hours.

To further combat the wet and cold morning weather conditions, Charlie would wear cotton gloves. Although the main purpose of wearing cotton gloves was to minimise finger bruising (on the susceptible skins of Granny Smith apples), he also wore them as a means to keep his hands warm, but this was largely ineffective as the gloves would quickly be soaked due to the overly damp conditions. Several times during the morning, Charlie would take his gloves off and attempt to wring as much water out of them as possible. The gloves, however, did offer some protection whenever he was handling the icy steel ladders, which were coated in ice for the first hour or so.

Charlie soon discovered an effective way to keep his hands warm during the cold, wet and icy conditions. He would keep the tractor engine running; regularly put his hands near the exhaust pipe in an attempt to maintain free movement of the fingers!

In the last week of May, the last of the Granny Smith apples at Comeforth Orchard were removed from the trees. The Breezer family (Ernie, Daphne, and their son Jethro) were grateful that Charlie stuck it out to the bitter end and, subsequently, offered him future fruit-picking employment in their orchard: cherries, stone fruits, and (of course) apples.

In the ensuing fruit-picking seasons, Charlie's main source of employment was in Kevin and Alan's orchard. He would, however, work on Comeforth Orchard on numerous occasions, primarily as a means to fill in any gap periods of employment. Thus, in future fruit-picking seasons, Charlie was able to achieve relatively full employment from mid-December to the end of May via these two orchards.

The past few months had enabled Charlie to acquire a substantial pool of valuable information regarding the fruit/vegetable harvest seasons – especially throughout the eastern states of Australia. He, originally, had planned to travel northwards to seek employment in the state of Queensland to experience the 'winter sun' (warmer winter temperatures). Jed and others, though, managed to convince him to firstly explore the Sunraysia area of Victoria (750-800 kilometres southwest of Orange) for the upcoming citrus season.

As May was about to come to a close, Charlie was back on the road again. After a ten-hour road trip, he arrived in the monotonously quiet Sunraysia town of Bangilot: sixty kilometres south of the city of Mildura.

3

Sunraysia Misery to Citrus in the Sun

On a bleakish and grey-skied afternoon in late May, Charlie arrived at the caravan park, two kilometres from the sleepy Victorian town of Bangilot. Located about 60 kilometres southeast of Mildura, Bangilot is part of the ill-defined District of Sunraysia. Often referred to (incorrectly) as an economic region, Sunraysia is located in north-western Victoria and south-western New South Wales.

Before entering the caravan park office, Charlie noticed a large French flag hoisted on a flagpole, swaying effortlessly in the gentle breeze, high above the dilapidated tiled roof. Inside the office, he was greeted by a petite-sized woman: Marie. Charlie enquired whether there was a vacant caravan or not.

French-born Marie was soon joined by her husband, Claude, an equally height-deprived gentleman but of a solidly-built frame. They were both aged in their mid-60s. A few minutes later, Claude led Charlie to a massive-sized caravan (32 feet in length). This would be his home for the next six weeks.

For the next few days, it mostly rained. Charlie, therefore, didn't bother seeking any citrus-picking employment. As it turned out, he didn't need to – work would practically come to him. Due to the then inclement weather, all of the caravan park dwellers were not working.

These washed-out days provided an opportunity for Charlie to meet some of the caravan park residents, mostly via 'competitive' card games such as euchre, 500, and poker. These social card games were mainly held in 'Dapper' Don's (a veteran itinerant worker aged in his late-fifties) caravan. Charlie soon discovered that his fellow itinerant workers were quite a motley crew of individuals!

Once the inclement weather had subsided, most of the itinerants were soon working in the orange orchards. Charlie's first employer was based near the nearby town of Iwrek (11 kilometres from Bangilot). By the third day, it soon became apparent to him that this particular employment venture would not be overly profitable. Over the next few weeks, Charlie would be employed by several different employers. None of them would prove to be financially beneficial.

The erratic wintry weather (plentiful rainfall combined with cool to cold conditions) was ever-persistent throughout Charlie's six-week stay in the area. Working in any wet conditions within this region was largely deemed as *un-Australian*. A few itinerant orange-pickers would attempt to toil away in the rain but they were soon met with 'union-like' peer pressure. Meanwhile, hotel establishments were well patronised on these washed-out days. Alternatively, Don's caravan would be abuzz with highly competitive card games.

The caravan park residency revealed an interesting array of diverse personalities, commencing with Charlie's next-door neighbour: Rufus. Scruffy in appearance, with long mangled and unwashed hair, a bushranger-type beard, and untidily attired, Rufus mostly lived life like a hermit.

Every few hours, Rufus would emerge from his caravan, taking his pet pooch (a dingo/kelpie cross) for a short stroll, either within the caravan park or along Craniathorpe Road (which ran along in front of the caravan park). On the odd occasion, he would walk with his dog to the Bangilot General Store to stock up on food items – mainly canned food. Rufus would then return to the caravan park with a dog leash in one hand and the handle of an antiquated trolley in the other one.

Steadfastly anti-social, Rufus would not converse with anyone – except with Claude – but only on the odd occasion. He would spend most of his time inside his caravan. Whenever Charlie passed by Rufus' caravan the television would be quite loud. Perhaps, he had a hearing problem. Additionally, the smell of a distinct well-known illegal substance would waft into the open air, via an opened window and also through the opened doorway!

Charlie would later learn from Claude that Rufus hadn't worked in years and he was a recipient of an invalid pension, largely due to ongoing mental issues. Whenever Charlie greeted Rufus with a simple hello, he was always met with the same response: a distinct scowl on his face; a slight nod of the head; and, accompanied by a few unintelligible caveman-like grunts and groans.

During his stay in the caravan park, Charlie would mostly be on amicable terms with most of the other residents. One particular itinerant resident, Italian-born Luigi (aged in his early sixties), however, would irk him regularly. Distinctly lacking any modesty, Luigi would frequently boast about his past speed-related fruit picking feats, regularly boasting, 'Pound for pound … I'm simply the best around!' Generally, the majority of the itinerant residents (especially the veteran ones) would just simply try to ignore him most of the time.

Luigi's regular obnoxious behaviour, especially after a substantial intake of alcohol, would occasionally lead to fiery verbal confrontations with other itinerants. At some point, he would attempt to provoke or initiate a physical altercation. Luigi's potential adversaries, who were generally younger, however, were reluctant to physically react to him – largely due to his small stature and advancing years.

Luigi's face bore the scars of numerous past physical encounters. Don, who had known him for at least two decades, informed all and sundry that Luigi, when involved in pugilistic disagreements, mostly came off second best!

Amongst the male-dominated itinerant community, there were two females: Brazilian-born Darlene and Cathy. Both of them were from the Gold Coast region of Queensland. The two women, aged in their mid-twenties, were travelling around Australia together via an itinerant lifestyle.

Luigi attempted to *woo* the pair by regularly inviting them into his caravan. They only went to his caravan on two occasions: both times for a 'Sunday roast' meal. Amicability between Luigi and the ladies didn't last for long – souring when he began making sexual advances toward them. Darlene, on many occasions, calmly reminded Luigi, 'Stop dreamin' … it will never happen!' Both of them soon limited any verbal contact with him.

Darlene and Cathy shared a large caravan. As the two lone females in the caravan park, they soon received an abundance of attention – especially from the younger itinerant male residents. The older itinerant males soon had a name for these youngsters – the 'Sniffer Brothers'.

The very attractive (and busty) Darlene, though, soon became sexually involved with *three* of the young males. One night, Charlie crossed paths with Cathy, who was shuffling somewhat despondently along the roadway in front of his caravan. Gently, he asked her if she was okay. After a brief discussion, Charlie invited Cathy to his caravan for a hot beverage as she didn't drink alcohol. Inside Charlie's caravan, Cathy explained to him that she had been locked out of her caravan as Darlene was having a vigorous romp with one of the 'Sniffer Brothers'!

Cathy further explained to Charlie that she had been previously locked out of the caravan on several occasions, whilst Darlene was providing 'physical comforting' (Cathy's words) to one of these three young males. That evening, the pair chatted for several hours. Whilst it soon emerged that neither of them 'fancied' each other sexually, a healthy friendship soon blossomed between the two. Over the next two weeks, Cathy would be a regular visitor to Charlie's caravan – she would be locked out of her caravan three or four nights per week.

One night, an intoxicated Luigi knocked on the security screen door of Charlie's caravan. He had also brought a six-pack of beer with him. Charlie quietly greeted Luigi but he refused to let him into the caravan. As he (Luigi) knew Cathy was inside the caravan, he asked her on several occasions, 'Hello princess… are you OK?'

Cathy tried to ignore Luigi's *inquisitive empathy* but in an exasperated manner, she eventually replied, 'I'm fine … enjoying Charlie's hospitality!'
Charlie quickly retorted, 'Goodnight Luigi – sleep well.'

Eventually, Cathy did hook up with one of the younger itinerant males one evening. One night, just after 8.00 pm, there was a knock on the security screen door of Charlie's caravan. It was Darlene! Sporting a wide cheeky grin, she casually explained to Charlie that Cathy had locked her out of the caravan and then, politely, asked him if she could stay in his caravan for several hours. Somewhat sheepishly, Charlie opened the security screen door and Darlene hastily made her way inside – with a bottle of red wine.

Over the next two hours, Darlene and Charlie chatted incessantly – over several glasses of wine. Suddenly, she stopped talking and gazed, unnervingly, at him. Then, Darlene reached into one of her jean pockets and pulled out a condom! A nervous Charlie was somewhat reluctant, as he was well aware of Darlene's recent bouts of promiscuity. Quickly sensing his insecurities, Darlene informed Charlie that she had recently been to a medical clinic (in the city of Mildura), adding that she was clean of any sexual diseases.

Sexually aggressive Darlene then led Charlie to his bed and forcibly pushed him onto it. She quickly removed all her clothes, revealing a solidly-built and curvy body frame. Moments later, Darlene was sitting on Charlie's chest, beaming directly down into Charlie's eyes. 'Thank you for looking after my friend Cathy and as a token of appreciation, I'm going to fulfil you with a night of sexual pleasure!'

Darlene stayed the entire night with Charlie. In the morning, the pair awoke to the heavy pitter-patter of raindrops, belting against the roof of the caravan. The torrential rain would continue for several hours. A short time later, he prepared breakfast for her. She stayed with him for a further two hours.

Just after midday, Charlie crossed paths with Don and Luigi near the amenities block. With a broad grin, Don coyly suggested to Charlie, 'I hear through the grapevine that you had an *interesting* night.'

Charlie slyly replied, 'Maybe!'

Luigi remained quiet – and surlily forlorn.

Although Charlie was amidst an interesting array of personalities, possibly the most intriguing one of them all was Claude. During the day and evenings, he would stroll (or patrol) along the roadways within the caravan park. Charlie would converse with Claude on an almost-daily basis and, thus, he soon learnt a lot about his colourful past.

Whilst strolling around within the confines of the caravan park, Claude always wore a distinct military-styled green beret. One day, Charlie decided to quiz him on the significance of this beret. Claude proudly declared to him that the beret represented his time when he served in the 2nd Foreign Parachute Regiment of the French Foreign Legion: a military service branch of the French Army.

Although Claude had been living in Australia for over twenty years, he still had a 'heavy' French accent. Charlie, along with other caravan park residents, soon realised that he (Claude) was still a patriotic Frenchman. Somewhat amusingly, the sound of the French national anthem, *La Marseillaise*, would seep from the office building each morning – easily audible to nearby residents. Charlie could mentally picture Claude standing in the lounge room – proudly saluting the French flag, draped across one of the walls.

Claude, generally, was quite a pleasant and peaceful character, but he (occasionally) had a *short-fused* temper. Claude had a strict rule for visitors: leave the caravan park by 9.00 pm sharp. Every evening, just before 9.00 pm, he would be seen wandering throughout the caravan park grounds – with a baseball bat.

One particular Friday evening, Claude confronted a group of young males in a caravan, who had been drinking copious amounts of alcohol for several hours. He informed three of them that visiting times ceased at 9.00 pm and it was time for them to vacate the premises. Two of the young lads, on seeing the baseball bat in Claude's hands, casually made their way to a vehicle in the visitors' parking lot.

The third male, who was partially stoned on marijuana (and affected by alcohol as well), challenged Claude and refused to leave. A loud verbal confrontation soon erupted, easily heard throughout the caravan park. Charlie and others emerged from their caravans to investigate the noisy commotion but no one would intervene. Ronald, one of the veteran itinerants, casually predicted that Claude is going to whack the obnoxious brat with the baseball bat. He was right!

The young male became more and more abusive and frequently voiced profanities. Although Claude mostly responded in English, he occasionally uttered the words *Sacrebleu* and *Mon Dieu*. The youngster still refused to leave and eventually, Claude declared, 'This is gonna hurt!'

Claude then struck him in the legs with the baseball bat (with reasonable force) and the young lad immediately collapsed to the ground in pain. He was no longer uttering vile profanities! Unable to walk properly, the obnoxious youngster was assisted to the visitors' car park and placed in a waiting vehicle. The vehicle then sped away from the caravan park.

Twenty minutes later, a police vehicle drove up and stopped beside Claude, who was talking to several of the caravan park residents. A young constable, who was probably not long out of cadet school, nervously alighted from the passenger side of the vehicle. Moments later, the senior officer casually emerged from the driver's side. The senior officer directed the caravan park residents to move away from Claude.

For the next ten minutes or so, the senior officer was engaged in a quiet discussion with Claude. The young constable was noticeably silent. Then, the senior officer shook Claude's hand and gave him a pat on the back. Just before the officers re-entered their vehicle, the senior officer loudly quipped, 'Claude, if you have any future problems with the *inmates* – just let us know.'

After residing in the Bangilot Caravan Park for six weeks, Charlie decided it was time to relocate to 'sunny' Queensland. The wet and cold wintery conditions had largely resulted in sporadic work conditions. He had not saved much money from the six-week employment venture. He had managed, though, to bank nearly $2000 – solely due to successful punting on racehorses.

Charlie departed the Sunraysia region and began the long arduous journey north to the state of Queensland. Destination: the town of Gayndah. On the way, Charlie decided to stay in the city of Orange (New South Wales) for several days. Whilst there, he decided to purchase various items of camping equipment: a large canvas tent (with a steel frame); a foldup outdoor dining setup; a gas cooker with hotplates; a medium-sized gas bottle; and, a large esky/cooler box.

Before departure, Charlie converted the rear section of his station wagon into a 'bedroom'. With the back bench seat folded down, he was able to fit in a double-sized mattress.

Curtains were then installed, covering the rear side windows and the back window. When travelling, the curtains were opened and camping equipment (and luggage) was placed on the covered double-sized mattress. Whilst staying in a caravan park (or on an orchard), Charlie would sleep in the vehicle. The large canvas tent was used as a 'dining' area and for luggage storage.

On an icy and foggy morning, Charlie drove out of Orange and along the Mitchell Highway towards the city of Dubbo. It was mid-July. Fourteen hours and 1120 kilometres later, he arrived in Gayndah (in the North Burnett Region). For the next three nights, Charlie stayed in one of the local caravan parks, situated on the Burnett River.

Over the next two days, Charlie explored the local environs of Gayndah, which included a considerable amount of time in one of the town's hotels. As a means to gather information concerning localised employment opportunities, he would engage in quite a few *intriguing* conversations. Unfortunately for Charlie, he soon found himself in meaningless conversations with two local 'misfits'.

The local misfits lacked basic social skills or any form of social etiquette. In future travels, Charlie would often come across these types of people. As compulsive utterers of *fabricated drivel,* these individuals would often seek victims in the false hope that their irritating (and irrational) behavioural traits would be tolerated!

Charlie, nevertheless, soon learnt that there was a plentiful supply of employment available in many of the orange orchards in the districts of Gayndah, Mundubbera, and Eidsvold. Unfortunately, many of these orchards did not offer itinerant workers any accommodation facilities. Instead, hotels or caravan parks were the only options available.

Fortunately, Charlie did manage to obtain an address of an orange orchard (25 kilometres from Gayndah) which provided a tract of land containing numerous powered sites. The itinerant worker, though, still needed to have their own means of accommodation such as a caravan, motorhome, or tent.

After driving along an unsealed and corrugated road for about ten kilometres, Charlie arrived at a large packing shed. After a brief discussion with one of the orchard's owners, he was directed to the accommodation area. The accommodation area was well maintained and consisted of powered sites and an amenity block (including laundry facilities). In the middle of the self-accommodation area was a decades-old homestead – surrounded by an enclosed porch.

After pitching his tent, Charlie soon met the lone occupant of the homestead: Errol. A bespectacled, middle-aged Aboriginal man, he had been living in the ageless dwelling for over twenty years. Errol was employed on this orange orchard all year round. Besides picking oranges, he would undertake other orcharding tasks: pruning fruit trees; chemical spraying (fertilisers, for example); and, irrigation laying/maintenance. During the upcoming orange-picking season, Errol would ensure that the homestead's lounge area would be a regular buzz of social activity as he was quite hospitable to the 'itinerant worker collective'.

As there was a shortage of tractors in this orchard, it was necessary for two or three people to work together. Each tractor, however, had five bin trailers. There were three large wooden bins on each trailer. The orchard's terrain was largely 'levelled' (i.e. with a flat even surface) and there was plenty of space between the rows of orange trees. From a safety point of view, it was relatively easy to manoeuvre the tractor throughout the orchard – even when all fifteen wooden bins were full of oranges.

For the first two days of the orange-picking season, Charlie worked with two local lads: Paul and Michael. On both days, the fifteen bins were filled with oranges. Charlie, though, felt that he was probably filling six or seven of them!

At the end of the second day, Errol approached Charlie and *politely insisted* that he should work with him. Charlie suspected that the orchard management wanted him to share the tractor (Errol had worked on his own for the first two days). Knowing that Errol was an experienced orange picker (and a fast one as well), he was initially reluctant to work with him. The following day, the pair filled *all* fifteen bins. Charlie was exhausted!

Throughout the season, Charlie would obtain a lot of useful tips from Errol about orange-picking. As a result, his earning capacity rapidly improved. Every day, the pair would consistently fill 15-18 bins of oranges.

Away from the working environment, Charlie would occasionally socialise with some of the other orchard-dwelling itinerants. The majority of the campsite dwellers were mainly middle-aged (or older) retired/semi-retired couples and singles who had relinquished an urban life: resigning or retiring from white/blue-collar jobs. In exchange, they had decided to choose a nomadic and carefree itinerant lifestyle.

Throughout the orange-picking season, Charlie would regularly converse with a family of five: mum and dad, along with their two sons and daughter. They were originally from the northern seaside suburb of Narrabeen (Sydney, NSW).

The father of the clan retired from the legal profession, once all three of his offspring had completed high school. The family group then decided to travel throughout Australia, via a working itinerant lifestyle. At the time, they were in their third year of travelling, moving from place to place in two vehicles (each towing a caravan). On the orchard, the two sons worked together on one tractor, whilst the other three worked together on another tractor. Between the five of them, they would generally pick between 35-40 bins of oranges each day.

Charlie remained on the orchard for seven weeks as the availability of work was relatively steady: five or six days each week. Whilst weather conditions were generally favourable (i.e. mostly rain-free), there were several late starts, courtesy of a substantial amount of morning dew. Orchard management did not want any oranges removed from the trees whilst the rind was quite damp.

Outside work hours, life on the orchard was generally amiable, as everyone seemingly got on quite well with each other. Light-hearted, friendly chitchat dominated the general conversation within the campsite community. A major disruption to this wondrous communal experience, however, was the occasional unwelcomed presence of feral cats!

On several occasions, one of the itinerant campsite residents (Colin) would grab his rifle. Chasing after them, he would shoot indiscriminatingly in their direction, as a means to discourage them from approaching the camping area. But none of the feral cats were ever shot – they quickly anticipated any looming danger. Although the feral felines were more active at night, all food items had to be securely kept away from them at all times.

As a precaution, Charlie kept all non-refrigerated food items in the rear section of his vehicle, instead of inside the tent. Each night, he would sleep on the comfortable double-sized mattress; the curtains were pulled across to block out any light. Additionally, Charlie would leave the driver-side window down a few centimetres to allow some fresh air into his vehicle.

As Charlie was sleeping one night, he was awoken by a strange noise. Something was moving around on the front bench seat of the vehicle. In a dazed stupor, Charlie grabbed a nearby steering wheel lock, fearing that there might be a snake slithering around on the front seat. Cautiously, he turned on a torch (flashlight) and then shone it into the front section of the car.

Suddenly, there was a horrible shriek – a feral cat. It *frantically* tried to make its way quickly back out through the narrow-gapped driver's side window. As it was a cold night, Charlie believed that the feral feline may have just been looking for a warm sleeping place. He was now wide awake! For the remainder of the night, Charlie did not sleep very well. Needless to say, in the ensuing nights, he would only leave the driver's side window down – no more than one centimeter.

Charlie recounted the nightly incident to Errol the next morning. Quietly chuckling, he stated to Charlie that he had had similar encounters on many occasions over the years.

Errol further added, despite numerous efforts to implement effective measures in securing the house each night, these unwanted intruders could be quite determined, squeezing through the narrowest of gaps or openings.

During his stay in this orchard, Charlie would gain useful information concerning the numerous fruit/vegetable harvest seasons, in and around many towns and cities, located within the state of Queensland: Gatton (the Lockyer Valley region); the Gympie region; the Bundaberg region; and, in the North Queensland towns of Ayr, Gumlu, Guthalungra, and Bowen.

Charlie had intended to seek employment in the Lockyer Valley region (over 300 kilometres south of Gayndah) after the completion of the orange picking. But he was soon made aware of unsavoury work practices in this particular area – especially during the onion-harvest season. For example, a large group (of a particular ethnicity) would arrive at an onion farm between 3.00 am and 4.00 am. Via the use of lighting from car headlights and/or other forms of light, the group would have the whole crop of onions picked (harvested) by 7.00 am or 8.00 am! Local or itinerant onion pickers would arrive at the farm, only to discover that they had *no employment* for that day.

Charlie decided to venture, therefore, northwards to tropical North Queensland, north of the Tropic of Capricorn. Several of his co-workers had pre-arranged employment in the Burdekin Shire (which included the towns of Bowen, Gumlu, Guthalungra, and Ayr) whilst they were still on the orange orchard.

Before departing the North Burnett Region, Charlie was given an address of a tomato-growing farm located about 30 kilometres inland from the town of Bowen. He was assured that obtaining employment at this particular tomato farm would pose no problem. Additionally, the owners of the tomato farm also provided a choice of accommodation facilities. Besides a campsite (with powered sites), there was a large house. The house had multiple rooms which had been converted into individual living quarters.

The past seven weeks had been quite profitable for Charlie. Instead of driving directly to the town of Bowen (a distance of 920 kilometres) he, firstly, decided to have a ten-day holiday.

After departing from the orchard, Charlie drove his vehicle eastwards to the city of Maryborough. He stayed there for three days.

For the remaining seven days, Charlie casually drove northwards along the Bruce Highway. Along the way, he stayed overnight in the towns of Gin Gin, Bororen, and Seventeen Seventy (and for two nights in the cities of Bundaberg and Rockhampton). Charlie arrived in the *mystical tropical paradise* of Bowen in the mid-afternoon.

4

The Party Farm

After travelling north from the city of Rockhampton for over six hours (and 520 kilometres), Charlie arrived at the southern outskirts of the coastal town of Bowen in the mid-afternoon. It was late August. Bowen (formerly known as Fort Denison) was the site of the first settlement in North Queensland. It was established in 1861.

Charlie was greeted with pleasant and warm weather conditions, exacerbated by beaming rays of sunshine. A lovely winter's day! The warm conditions prompted him to wear typical summer attire: shorts, a singlet (vest), and a pair of thongs (flip-flops).

The journey from Rockhampton to Bowen was quite a boring trip for Charlie – especially the section of the Bruce Highway commonly known as the 'Marlborough Stretch.' The Marlborough Stretch spans between the city of Rockhampton and the town of Sarina, a distance of just over 300 kilometres. This section of highway virtually bypassed all the small townships. The scenery throughout the journey was consistently non-picturesque: brown withered grasslands and grey lifeless trees (and leaf-free) – made worse with the occasional sighting of malnourished 'poverty-stricken' cattle.

The Marlborough Stretch had been known by several other names in the past – the 'Horror Stretch' was one of them. In previous decades there had been a high percentage of fatigue-related accidents and deaths. Before the completed upgrade (a significant one) of the Bruce Highway in 1985 between Sarina and Rockhampton, the road was practically a one-lane highway.

Trucks/lorries, generally, had the *right away* as other vehicles needed to drive along the dirt sections whilst the trucks continue along the sealed section of the road. It was worse for truck drivers, however, when they had to pass other trucks. The loss of large side mirrors was a common occurrence! For motorists, it was also advisable to wind up the car windows each time they passed a vehicle, to prevent large clouds of reddish-brown dust from filling the interior of the vehicle.

There was another reason – a sinister one – as to why this stretch of highway was known as the 'Horror Stretch.' Before the major upgrading of this section of highway, there had been quite a long history of unsavoury incidents. Robberies and assaults were rife at times, but even worse – several cases of multiple murders.

Another colloquial name for this stretch of highway was the *Crystal Highway*, due to a significant number of vehicle windscreens being either severely damaged or disintegrating on impact. The main culprits were the large trucks hurtling up-and-down the one-lane highway – spraying stones or rocks randomly at passing vehicles.

When Charlie reached the southern outskirts of Bowen, the fuel gauge was showing that his vehicle was perilously low on fuel. Fortunately, a petrol service station soon loomed into view. The owner refilled the vehicle with fuel and soon introduced himself as André. The service station also had a small restaurant and Charlie decided to have a sit-down meal. Whilst consuming his meal, he soon struck up an amicable conversation with André.

André, along with his wife and two young children, dwelled in a small house at the rear of the petrol service station. He revealed to Charlie that his family had owned this business for the past two years, having emigrated from France to Australia several years beforehand.

After consuming his meal, Charlie asked André for directions to Donny Freeman's tomato farm, located 30 kilometres southwest of Bowen. A short time later, he was driving along the Bruce Highway once more. At the time, the highway in this particular area was under construction. It mainly consisted of a corrugated (courtesy of numerous large trucks driving back and forth on it) and gravel surface. Two kilometres from central Bowen, Charlie turned left, continuing along the Bruce Highway.

Just before this highway turnoff, motorists (and passengers) would be greeted with the abysmal sight of salt mines. Upon viewing this landscape *eyesore*, it would be quite understandable for potential tourists/travellers to just continue along the highway – bypassing the coastal town of Bowen altogether. Years later, very large billboards, containing posters of Bowen's idyllic and wondrous beaches, gracefully welcomed everyone to the area, effectively blocking the view of the ghastly salt mines.

Several minutes later, Charlie turned left into Collinsville Road (later renamed the Bowen Development Road) and drove along this road for about fifteen kilometres. Charlie then turned left onto Mount Dangerous road. At first, the road was sealed but it soon disintegrated into corrugated gravel. But worse was to follow. As he got closer to his destination, Charlie drove through rocky streams (which, fortunately, were mostly water-free) and along needless windy dirt tracks. The rugged terrain was far more suitable for four WD driving – not for an aging HQ Holden station wagon.

When André was giving directions (to the tomato farm), he informed Charlie that once he could smell the piggery, the packing shed was close by. Eventually, an unpleasant and quite overwhelming smell did indeed enter Charlie's nasal cavity! After driving past the piggery, he soon arrived at the entrance of a large packing shed.

After alighting from his vehicle, Charlie walked onto an elevated platform. A middle-aged woman approached and greeted him. Instantly, Mary (Donny Freeman's wife) asked Charlie if he was looking for tomato-picking employment. He replied in the affirmative.

Mary, in quite a gruff voice, informed Charlie that he could commence employment the next morning. She also suggested to him to bring out more people, if possible, as there were *numerous* vacancies. Alarm bells automatically began to ring in Charlie's head! It soon occurred to him that this particular tomato farm may have a high turnover of tomato pickers each season. A 'revolving gate' mentality towards its employees, perhaps?

Charlie then quizzed Mary on accommodation facilities. She informed him that there was a large accommodation area about two kilometres away. Charlie had already driven passed this site. It contained a large house, a few caravans, and several tents. Before he left, Mary told him to speak to the 'caretaker' and sarcastically quipped, 'Harry will help you … he's easy to find – he looks like Father Christmas.'

Charlie drove back along the track, covering his nose as he went past the piggery, in an attempt to avoid further damage to his sensitive paranasal sinuses. A few minutes later, Charlie arrived at the accommodation site and parked his vehicle near a large nineteenth-century farm mansion. It was surrounded by an enclosed porch area.

'Christmas Father' Harry was on the front porch – in a wooden rocking chair – with a cigarette in one hand and a bottle of XXXX beer in the other hand. His long wiry silvery-white hair, along with a full-faced beard (of similar colour proportions), blended in quite well with his 'Grateful Dead' singlet!

Before any discussion took place, Charlie's first impression of Harry was that this was someone still trying to live in the psychedelic era of the late-1960s and early-1970s. Judging by his appearance, Charlie thought that Harry was probably in the 50+ age category. He would soon learn, however, that the silvery-white-haired gentleman had just celebrated his 41st birthday! Nevertheless, Charlie introduced himself and upon a reciprocal greeting, Harry gave him a cold bottle of XXXX beer and a milk crate to sit on.

Despite appearances, Charlie soon realised that Harry was quite a pleasant and peaceful chap, with a general carefree attitude towards life. In future fruit-picking seasons (in the states of Queensland and Victoria), the pair would cross paths on several occasions.

Originally from inner-city Melbourne (Victoria), Harry had now been part of the itinerant lifestyle for over ten years. He soon informed Charlie that this particular tomato farm was, basically, a *party farm*. During previous seasons, there had been a substantially large turnover of tomato pickers. He further added that earning a reasonable income would prove difficult on this tomato farm as the amount of employment available each week (typically between 20-30 hours) could be quite sporadic.

The farm 'mansion' had numerous rooms (catering for single, double, or twin shares) with a capacity for up to twenty people. The house contained a large kitchen area (which was also used by the tent dwellers), a large bathroom, and washing facilities. There was also a separate amenities block, near the powered sites, which was mainly used by the caravan and tent dwellers.

Charlie was informed that there had been no work on the tomato farm for the past three days. Nearly all the resident itinerants were in town (Bowen). According to Harry, the 'Aussies' and 'Kiwis' (Australians and New Zealanders) were in one of the town's hotels, whilst the European backpackers could be found on one of Bowen's glorious beaches.

Harry led Charlie to a vacant single room that only comprised of a bed frame and a well-used mattress. This would be his home for the next two weeks. Charlie noticed that the misshapen mattress had broken bedsprings poking into it. The solution: drag the mattress onto the floor. The dilapidated bedframe would be used to accommodate some of his belongings, namely a large backpack and some of the camping equipment.

That evening, all and sundry had returned to the accommodation site and were gathered around a large open fire. Before darkness had crept in, Harry had created a fireplace with suitably-sized fallen tree branches. Adding old newspapers and using a cigarette lighter, the fire was soon well alight.

Aided by moderate quantities of alcohol and recreational smoked substances, the mood of the general conversation could be best described as *excitable*. By 11.00 pm, though, the overall noise level had virtually subsided to one of a stifled murmur. Most folks were blissfully sound asleep.

The next morning, just after 7.00 am, the 'excitable' tomato-picking crew were gathered at a nearby field. Several blocks of tomatoes were ready to be picked. Charlie had learnt the previous night that a sizeable number of the group (including him) had never indulged in tomato-picking before. Martin, the paddock foreman, then proceeded to provide a five-minute crash course on how to pick tomatoes *correctly*.

Each tomato-picker was instructed to do the following: only fill the buckets with tomatoes that had some colour tinge of red/pink on the skin; the unripened green tomatoes were to remain on the bushes; and, the soft (overripe) red tomatoes were supposed to be thrown in the 'alley' lanes (between the rows of tomato plants).

Within the first few days, Charlie soon learnt a few tricks of the tomato-picking 'game' from several itinerant fruit pickers. Harry and Chan (a Chinese-Malay national), in particular.

Chan had been an itinerant fruit picker in Australia for over five years and was officially (for taxation purposes) known as *Johnny Martin*. He had a TFN (tax file number) that matched the fictional name, issued by the Australian Taxation Department. At the time, an individual would be given a TFN when they completed their first tax return. As a result, numerous TFNs were issued to people with fictitious names! Later, an individual had to apply for a TFN and provide adequate identification to be granted one.

Several key 'tricks' that Charlie had learnt on the first picking day included: tilt the bucket towards the selected tomatoes to be picked; place the bucket between one's legs and quickly throw the tomatoes (don't place them) into the bucket; only throw some of the soft red tomatoes into the alley lanes; and, fill the bottom half of the bucket with a mixture of soft red tomatoes and blemished tomatoes. The top part of the bucket was to be filled with 'quality' tomatoes. Each individual tomato-picker was paid by the number of full buckets of tomatoes (i.e. by piece rate). Martin *never* conducted bucket checks.

By the end of the third day, Charlie's daily tally was one of the highest within the tomato-picking group. It soon, however, emerged that Chan was the fastest tomato-picker. As a means to counteract the often tedious and largely repetitive nature of the work, Charlie's daily goal was to try and keep pace with him as much as possible.

Charlie soon discovered that a 'mind-over-matter' approach to tomato picking was highly necessary. This *back-breaking* mode of employment certainly tested one's physical capabilities – and pain threshold. One would soon experience a high level of discomfort within the lower back and in the top part of one's legs (thigh and hamstring muscles mostly). After being bent over in a forward direction for a substantial amount of time, Charlie soon discovered that straightening his body was, at times, quite an arduous task!

Charlie's bulky frame was probably better suited to picking fruit from trees (apples, pears, oranges, etc.), compared to ground-picking employment. Although tomato-picking was quite taxing on Charlie's body, nevertheless, it didn't discourage him from returning to the Bowen region – for twelve more seasons. This type of employment, however, inevitably led to Charlie experiencing future back/spinal problems. Extensive physiotherapy would later be required.

On this particular tomato farm, several of the group (including Charlie) were trying to earn a decent income from this 'entrepreneurial pursuit'. The majority, however, were more interested in other aspects of the 'experience': the free accommodation; the nightly, party-like atmosphere get-togethers around the open fire; developing or enhancing their suntans; and, filling their travelling diaries with daily handwritten entries.

The European female backpackers were an intriguing lot. Largely due to their dress sense, especially when they were on one of Bowen's idyllic beaches (often braless and only wearing a G-string), they collectively became known as the *G-String Sisters*. Their two key objectives were to earn enough money to fund their weekly expenses and to indulge in the daily ritual of developing or enhancing their suntans!

Petra (from Austria), Inga (from Germany), Tina (from Belgium), and Linda (from the UK) casually toiled each day in the tomato fields. Each of them would wear a pair of shorts that revealed a certain amount of bum-cheek, a singlet, and lots of suntan lotion. It was quite apparent why several males (Harry, for example) enjoyed working on this farm – season after season.

Petra was certainly a favourite. As one of the quicker tomato-pickers, she would often be working ahead of most of the group. It didn't take long for certain alert males to realise that she wasn't wearing any underwear – and at times, provided an eyeful of her private parts.

During Charlie's two-week stay on this tomato farm, employment was quite sporadic; three days' work, then three days off, three days on, two days off, and then another three-day work stint. Worse was to follow though – seven days of no employment.

Charlie and Chan decided that it was time to seek *greener pastures*. They wanted to be employed on a tomato farm that could consistently provide five or six days of employment each week. Some itinerant workers ('Kiwi' Ken and 'Christmas Father' Harry for example) enjoyed the 'social camaraderie' on this tomato farm, along with the free accommodation. Neither of them appeared to be overly interested in the financial aspects of the tomato-picking experience. Charlie suspected that both of them were probably receiving fortnightly unemployment benefits as well!

'Kiwi' Ken also had another reason why he wanted to stay on Donny Freeman's tomato farm. He was sexually involved with Tina. Harry, meanwhile, was trying to become sexually involved – with any of the females in the tomato-picking group. He had earlier bragged to Charlie that he had experienced moderate success during past seasons and was quite content to just *keep trying*. For Charlie and Chan, though, the novelty of the 'party farm' had well and truly worn off and they soon found a more financially prosperous employment opportunity elsewhere.

5

Salt Mines and Beautiful Beaches

Charlie's newfound friend, Chan, soon discovered a new employment opportunity at another tomato farm: 15 kilometres north of Bowen. Unfortunately, this tomato farm did not provide any accommodation facilities. The pair, however, managed to secure caravan accommodation at Edgecombe Village Caravan Park (now named Bowen Holiday Park).

The caravan park was located four kilometres south of Bowen, near the petrol service station owned by Andre and his wife. As Chan did not have a vehicle, he needed to rely on Charlie for transport to and from the tomato farm. They decided to share a large, spacious caravan; accommodation (and petrol costs) would be equally shared. For the next two and a half months, Charlie and Chan consistently worked five or six days on any given week.

During Charlie's two-and-a-half-month stay at the caravan park, he would get to know the owner (Graham) quite well. Graham was short in stature but of a stocky build. He also sported a *garden gnome-like* beard. Amongst the caravan park residents, he was affectionately known as 'GG' (Garden Gnome) – a nickname he seemed to relish.

Enjoying the tropical sunshine, Graham would spend a considerable portion of his day with regular walks inside the confines of the caravan park. In stark contrast, his wife Beryl would rarely leave the office complex – except for the occasional shopping expedition to Bowen or other towns and cities within a 250-kilometre radius of Bowen.

Graham ensured that several key practices in the caravan park were strictly adhered to: all areas were to be consistently kept in a clean and tidy state; motorists were to drive within the caravan park at 'walking pace' only; and, noise levels were *always* to be at a tolerable level.

During the brighter hours of the day, Graham always wore dark sunglasses. The ferocious rays of the sun would beam down, mercilessly, on the white-sanded roadways. These ultra-bright fiendish rays, emitted from the road surface, would severely limit a person's eyesight at times. One's water-filled vision could be potentially blinding and painful.

Another major hazard was the ever-present plagued-like numbers of cane toads. A large proportion of this 'unwelcomed community' would meet a squishy end – largely due to coming in contact with the tires of moving vehicles. At times, the sandy-white thoroughfares were littered with these slimy (but mostly flattened) unwanted fiends. Most residents, when walking bare-footed or wearing thongs/flip-flops anywhere in the caravan park, soon learned that it was a good idea to constantly look *downwards*.

During times of fading light or darkness, a torch/flashlight was a necessary piece of equipment when strolling along any roadway or path. Cane toads that hadn't yet come in contact with a tire from a moving vehicle, were still hopping around aimlessly. Another hazard that required vigilance, was the odd snake lurking about – seeking a snack of cane toads.

Residents/holidaymakers with pets, especially small dogs, needed to be extra vigilant. They needed to ensure that their pets didn't come in contact with any poisonous toxins, ejected by spitting cane toads. Snakes were a lesser hazard. Graham enforced the rule that all dogs needed to be on a leash when being walked within the confines of the caravan park. A dog's bark, however, soon alerted its owner to any impending danger!

In the middle of the caravan park, there was a large communal area containing the following: wooden picnic-style tables with attachable bench seats; cooking facilities (a barbeque and several cooking hotplates); a large bench that contained a double-sink and dishwashing racks; two refrigerators; and, a television. Whilst this area was primarily for the tent-dwelling community, it would occasionally be an area of social interaction for other caravan park residents, as well.

Every night at 9.01 pm or 9.02 pm, Graham would casually stroll down from his residence (part of the office complex) to the communal area. With a large bright torch in his hand, he would politely request but with purposeful intent, that all noise needed to cease to a barely audible level – especially the volume of the television. However, as most users of the communal area needed to be awake by 6.00 am the following day, compliance with Graham's request was always met.

Yet again, Charlie would meet an array of colourful itinerant identities residing in the caravan park. Occasionally, he and Chan would venture to the 'isolated' tent-dwelling section, located well away from the office and other residential sites. The tenting community ensured that this area, outside work hours, would be regularly filled with the aromatic smell of cannabis!

As this tenting area was a reasonable distance from the caravan dwellers and those that lived in buses or motor homes, Graham largely chose to ignore this particular recreational activity. He did, however, impose a total ban on the use of any illegal substances within the communal area. Offenders were immediately evicted from the caravan park. On the other hand, Graham had no issues with alcohol or cigarette smoking in the communal area, provided that users put empty cans/bottles (or wine casks) and cigarette butts into one of the several garbage bins provided.

As there were numerous palm trees in the caravan, it was advisable to park your vehicle a sensible distance away from them – coconuts fell to the ground randomly. Chan's childhood 'skill' of climbing palm trees in his Malaysian homeland and knocking down the coconuts to the ground with his machete (yes, he travelled with one) soon caught Graham's attention! The fallen coconuts were later chopped into pieces for human consumption.

Despite being thirty-nine years old at the time, Chan *easily* ran up and down the trunks of the palm trees. Graham regularly asked him to knock down ripened or near-ripened coconuts with his machete. Chan would then be rewarded with a six-pack of bottled cold XXXX beers!

Outside employment hours, Chan would spend a large part of his spare time indulging in handicraft activities. He would either make bracelets, anklets, or chains (from small seashells, gems, cotton, or strips of leather) as a means of making extra income. Carrying a small leather bag with him at all times, Chan would regularly attempt to sell his wares practically anywhere: in the caravan park; on a tomato farm; in hotel establishments; and, even, at one of Bowen's picturesque beaches!

Another colourful identity was Ian who lived in a hired caravan next door to Charlie and Chan. Their first encounter with Ian occurred just after they had taken up residence in the caravan park. Early one morning, a sheepish Ian, still in an alcohol-affected stupor, approached the pair's caravan and gently tapped on the screen door.

'Have you got a spare teabag?' he politely asked.

'Yeah … sure,' replied Charlie.

Ian gingerly made his way back to his caravan. Two minutes later there was a knock on the side of Charlie and Chan's caravan.

'You wouldn't have any spare sugar by any chance?'

'Sure … how many teaspoons?' responded Charlie.

'Just the one.'

Charlie put a teaspoon of sugar in Ian's beverage-stained mug. Once more, he shuffled back to his caravan. Three minutes later, there was another gentle tap on the side of the van.

'Umm … do have any spare hot water?'

A reticent Charlie was about to respond, but an exasperated Chan blurted out, 'For fuck's sake Ian, why didn't you just ask us for a cup of tea… come inside and we'll make you a cuppa!'

Ian declined Chan's offer. As Charlie poured hot water into the beverage-stained mug, he claimed that the element in his jug had just gone 'kaput'.

At the time, Ian was working on a tomato farm located near Tootaloot Road, a ten-minute drive from the caravan park. As he didn't possess a vehicle, Ian would obtain a daily lift to and from the tomato farm with a tent-dwelling couple: Garth and Doreen. Each afternoon after work, they would be in Ian's caravan for several hours, discussing the days' events (mainly work-related) over a substantial intake of bottled cold beer.

Every Saturday (the standard non-work day in the region) the trio would venture into Bowen, via the local taxi service, just before midday. Many hours later, they would return to the caravan park before the night-time darkness had crept in. The taxi driver, however, would drop them off at the nearby service station so they could purchase hamburgers and cups of chips. Then they would trudge back to the caravan park. The staggering males would carry the food. Walking along fairly steadily, Doreen would carry a cardboard carton of beer (containing 24 bottles) on her shoulder!

Charlie and Chan soon realised that their new place of employment, near East Euri Creek Road, was a much better option than the previous one. For the next few weeks, the working week would mostly be a six-day one. Saturday was the day of rest. The day of arduous toil would commence around 7.00 am each morning (except for the last three weeks of the tomato-picking season where the starting time would be 6.00 am) and would come to a halt sometime between 2.00 pm–3.00 pm. On Sundays, along with many of the other tomato farms in the East Euri Creek area, tomato-picking would cease around 1.00 pm.

Charlie and Chan soon found themselves competing against several fast pickers; namely 'Kiwi' Neil, 'Spiderman' Matt, an Iranian-born couple (Ali and Rayna), and Czech-born George. Competition between the itinerant tomato pickers, whilst mostly jovial, could be quite fierce at times! Achieving the highest tally (total number of buckets of tomatoes picked) on any given day was an underlying *badge of honour*.

As Charlie pushed himself to his physical limitations (and beyond), he soon discovered that he had muscles – ones that had seldom been used in the past. In particular, Charlie's back was constantly stiff and sore. The painful discomfort was even worse after a hard day's toil – when the body began to cool down. Back at the caravan park, Charlie *enjoyed* taking a very warm shower, allowing the water to move up and down his spine for at least ten minutes in a sustained effort to ease the pain.

At times, in the late afternoon, there would be several caravan park residents having showers at the same time. It was easy to tell who the tomato pickers were – the water running down the back of each showering area, moving towards a single drain, was of a distinct green colour.

During work hours, the majority of tomato pickers worked bare-footed and did not wear gloves. As a consequence, an individual's hands and feet were primarily of green colour, mainly due to regular contact with the leaves of the tomato plant/bush. The use of ordinary soap had minimal effect in removing all hand and feet stains.

One of the better ways to remove the green stains was to cut a reasonably-sized green tomato in half. Next, use the green gel in the centre of the tomato to rub vigorously onto the hands and feet. Then add water to create a yellowish-green lather. This would remove most of the stains. Throughout the season, however, one would still have brown-coloured stain remnants on their hands and feet!

Away from the physical side of tomato-picking, a standard practice on the vast majority of tomato farms was the issuing of a 'tag bag' to each tomato picker. Each bag would contain a set of same-coloured plastic tags. Other tomato pickers would have sets of different coloured/patterned tags. After each bucket was filled with tomatoes a tag would be placed on the rim.

These tagged buckets would later be picked up by the *carters* who would carry and load them onto a nearby tray truck. Carting was heavy work but, financially, it was generally quite rewarding. The daily earnings of each carter depended on how many buckets they had loaded onto the tray truck and transported back to the packing shed. On some tomato farms, two or more carters would work together. At the end of the working day, they would either split the daily earnings equally or divide depending on the number of tray trucks (loaded with full buckets) transported back to the packing shed.

Each full bucket of tomatoes would weigh between 15-20 kilograms. Most carters would carry two buckets (one in each hand) to the tray truck, throughout the day. Some of these guys, though, would carry two buckets in each hand – but only for small periods. Carting 60-80 kilograms to a tray truck soon tested out one's physical limitations!

Carting 500-1000 buckets a day would be generally regarded as comfortable. Carting 1500-2000 (or more) buckets a day was much more physically demanding. Nevertheless, it was a great way for an individual to develop their fitness and strength levels – no need to pay for a rigorous gym workout.

On this tomato farm, there was just one carter. Bruce was heavily tattooed and of a thickset muscular build. He was mostly an affable chap but, at times, he could be quite a tumultuous character!

Aged in his early forties, Bruce had a rough weather-beaten face with numerous facial scars – along with numerous missing or badly chipped teeth. Charlie soon learnt that he had been in and out of jail a few times throughout his life. His motto *laws were made to be broken* ensured that he would be in regular contact with the local constabulary!

Bruce would openly brag to the tomato-picking crew that he had never had a boat licence or a fishing licence (which is only required for freshwater fishing). On most evenings, Bruce would be in his boat, fishing in saltwater or freshwater waterways. Using a large number of crab pots, he would snare a lot of mud crabs – illegally. Most of the illegal catch was sold to itinerant tomato pickers who, in turn, would pay Bruce either in cash, alcohol (cartons of beer), or plastic bags of marijuana. Over the next two months, Charlie and Chan would have a constant supply of mud crabs. They would reimburse Bruce each time with cartons of beer.

Before Charlie's first venture to North Queensland, the only seafood that he had ever consumed was crumbed or battered fish from a 'Fish and Chip' shop. During the tomato-picking season (the first of thirteen seasons), Charlie regularly snacked or feasted on a healthy variety of seafood: mud crabs, prawns, trevally, Spanish mackerel, red emperor, Moreton Bay bugs, etc.

Meanwhile, in the tomato paddock, Bruce could be quite a *pest* to the tomato-picking crew at times. During the first hour of the working day, his workload was quite light. Succumbing to a sense of ennui, he decided to annoy people. Firstly, he would drive the tray truck up to where an individual (or several people) were picking tomatoes on the outside rows of a block of tomatoes. Then he would stop the truck. Putting the gearbox in neutral, Bruce then proceeded to 'pump' the accelerator – emitting plenty of unpleasant-smelling diesel fumes.

Bruce thought the situation was hilarious. The recipient victims certainly didn't! In response, he soon found himself being pelted with plenty of rotten tomatoes – and the occasional empty bucket – purposely directed at his head. The driver's side window was always fully wound down.

The constant vigorous toil, combined with the incessant heat and high humidity, along with partial effects of daily alcohol (or marijuana) usage, would gradually take a heavy toll on Bruce – especially in the afternoons. If he dropped or stumbled over a bucket of tomatoes, Bruce would start growling (dog-like) or hiss angrily, cursing and swearing under his breath.

Occasionally, Bruce would bang his forehead (several times) on the side of the truck, yelling out, 'I hate this fuckin' job!'

Once the 'headbanging' session had ceased, Bruce would then take an audibly deep breath and calmly announce for all to hear.

'Now … that feels better!'

Bruce's abode of residence was about thirty kilometres south of the tomato farm. To get to and from work, he would drive his vehicle (a Holden Premier panel van with no number plates) along the ironically-named Bruce Highway. Driving erratically, Bruce would regularly do the following:

1. Drive well above the speed limit.
2. Overtake motorists on the *left* side of their vehicles (the side shoulders on some sections of the highway were quite wide).
3. Overtake on double yellow lines.
4. Never use the vehicle's indicators.
5. Constantly flash the high-beam headlights.
6. Zigzag (at a much slower speed) across *both* sides of the road.

Chan soon had a nickname for him – HB (Highway Bruce).

For over two decades, Bruce had been living in a wooden hut concealed within scrubland, close to a beach. Over several decades, his extended family (parents, aunts and uncles, offspring, siblings, siblings' offspring, his wife's family, etc) had built several wooden constructed dwellings – illegally and well concealed.

The local council (apparently) wasn't aware of the existence of these humble abodes for many years. When they did eventually become aware of them, no course of action was undertaken. The extended family had been known to local police for several decades due to their blatant and regular disregard for any laws or regulations. The popular consensus (according to the local inhabitants) was that the police and the local council seemed to be quite happy that the 'tribe' was well away from the local mainstream community!

As the tomato-picking season entered the middle of spring (mid-October), the volume of tomatoes to be picked had risen significantly. Demand for tomato pickers had significantly increased at most tomato farms.

Within the itinerant community, 'farm-swapping' soon became quite prevalent, purely as a means of attempting to increase one's earning capacity. As a result, bucket piece rates on many tomato farms increased; an element of a quasi-competition amongst the tomato growers soon took hold – as a means to secure a comfortable number of tomato-picking personnel.

Charlie and Chan's next-door neighbor (Ian) was also looking for another employment opportunity and he subsequently found one – on the tomato farm where they were working. As Ian didn't possess a vehicle, Charlie ended up with another passenger.

Ian would never pay any petrol money but he would provide Charlie and Chan with a cold bottle of beer at the end of each working day. From the first working day, Charlie firmly stated to him that he would need to be ready for work each morning, by waiting near his vehicle. He was not going to be Ian's alarm clock!

For the first week and a half, Ian went to work with Charlie and Chan each working day. No hassles. Then, one morning, a semi-intoxicated Ian gingerly entered Charlie's vehicle with an esky/icebox (which contained a bag of ice) and a carton of XXXX beer.

A bemused Charlie casually asked Ian what the occasion was.

'It's my 32nd birthday today,' he beamed and added, 'And I wish to celebrate it with my fellow tomato-pickers today!'

Before arriving at the tomato farm, Ian had already consumed two bottles of beer. After alighting from Charlie's vehicle, Ian proceeded to fill his esky with a dozen bottles of beer. His indiscreet escapade immediately caught the attention of the paddock boss (Alan).

Smirking, Alan bluntly asked, 'What's the occasion?'

'It's my birthday!'

'Are you going to do any work today?'

'Yeah… I'll be fine!'

At the time, alcohol (mainly beer) consumption and the usage of marijuana (smoking joints or the use of a bong) were commonplace during work hours! As long as people were working steadily, there were no issues with these types of practices.

For the first three hours, Ian worked quite well, having filled quite a reasonable number of buckets. During the half-hour morning break, the first of two half-hour breaks during the day, the majority of the tomato-picking crew (and Alan) each consumed a bottle of beer – 'assisting' Ian in the celebration of his birthday. After the morning break, everyone returned to work – except for Ian. His steady consumption of alcohol (since 5.30 am) was now affecting him!

Ian did not add to his morning tally of full buckets of tomatoes that day, but he did finish drinking the remaining bottles of beer in his esky! On the way back to the caravan park, Ian had fallen asleep in Charlie's vehicle. Once inside the caravan park, he had to be woken up. With some assistance from Chan, Charlie helped him to his caravan. A couple of hours later, Doreen and Garth were in Ian's caravan to further assist him in his birthday celebrations – another carton of beer.

The next morning, all was quiet in Ian's abode of residence. However, a pair of legs dangling out of the entrance of his caravan soon caught Charlie's attention. He casually wandered over towards Ian's caravan for a closer inspection. The dangling legs belonged to Doreen!

She was asleep on the floor – using an empty beer carton as a pillow. Garth was spread-eagled on the table on his back with arms and legs dangling over the sides. Charlie couldn't see Ian, but the sound of thunderous snoring from the rear of the caravan easily verified his whereabouts!

Ian decided to continue celebrating his birthday for the next few days and did not undertake any tomato picking. On the fourth day (of Ian's absence), paddock boss Alan politely informed Charlie that Ian's 'services' were no longer required!

As there were still numerous employment opportunities in the local region, Ian soon obtained employment at another tomato farm; one that was owned by Jerry 'Schizo' Plod. As there was a camping ground on this particular tomato farm, Ian decided to relocate there. The *camping facilities* included: a patch of land with plenty of trees for shade but no powered sites; a single hole-in-the-ground toilet; and, a small unused canal where the water was only suitable for personal bathing and washing clothes.

The last time Charlie crossed paths with Ian was inside one of Bowen's hotels. Already in a state of social inebriation, he was just filling in time waiting for a 4.00 pm appointment at a local medical centre. Charlie and Ian chatted amicably but at 3.50 pm, he promptly alighted from his stool. Ian shuffled unsteadily, with an intense sense of purpose, to the nearby medical centre!

Away from the treacherous drudge and toil of tomato picking, Charlie enjoyed a fulfilling social life. Meeting numerous fellow itinerants, he would stay in contact with many of them over the ensuing years. This social interaction also would ensure Charlie's 'membership' into a thriving itinerant fruit-picking network.

Possibly, one of the most intriguing aspects of Charlie's social life was the infamous *Sunday Sessions*. At the time, hotel establishments in the state of Queensland, on Sundays, were only opened between the hours of 11.00 am–1.00 pm (lunch) and 5.00 pm–7.00 pm (dinner). If 'entertainment' was provided, however, hotels could remain open from 11.00 am to 7.00 pm.

It was standard practice for the vast majority of tomato farms to cease work by 1.00 pm on Sundays. On this day, a large percentage of itinerant workers would occupy one of the several hotels in the town of Bowen. Those who were employed in the Euri Creek area or the Delta region, though, would congregate in the nearby town of Merinda (9km west of Bowen) between midday and 1.30 pm.

The Merinda Hotel would provide musical entertainment from 12.00 pm to 5.00 pm. Charlie and Chan would attend the Sunday Session nearly every Sunday. The music was primarily provided by makeshift bands. It soon became quite apparent, though, that there was a plentiful supply of talented musicians within the itinerant community! Several bands/groups would emerge from these Sunday Sessions and they, in turn, would perform at gigs within the local area and in other Queensland towns and cities, as well.

Note: [Two years later, new state government legislation enabled Queensland hotels to extend trading hours on Sundays, without having to provide entertainment].

The type of music played at the Merinda Hotel was predominantly either folk or blues-inspired (or a mixture of both), further enhanced with a melodic combination of guitars, drums, flutes, harmonicas, tambourines, etc. Whilst patrons were being treated to the music extravaganza, several large barbeques and roast spits were also in constant operation. A variety of meat-based meals, along with a variety of salads, were available and reasonably priced.

As most of the patrons arrived at this venue directly from the tomato paddock, the sight of green hands and green feet, along with tomato-stained work clothes, was quite prevalent. Amongst a colourful array of full-faced beards, long-flowing matted hairstyles, and friendship chains/bracelets, intertwined with the melodies of folk/blues-style music – Charlie felt that he was smack-bang in the middle of a bygone 1960s 'Hippy' Era. Nevertheless, it was still a great way to spend a Sunday afternoon!

Although hotel patronage from Monday-Thursday was generally well supported, Friday afternoons – especially from 4.00 pm, would be exceptionally busy. Most tomato farms were non-operational on Saturdays. The exuberant local social scene, therefore, would commence Friday afternoon and continue well into the night.

On Saturday afternoons, the hotels would also be well patronised, especially the ones that had TABs (betting agencies). A large portion of the itinerant community (and some of the residents as well) were avid weekly punters. They would mainly 'punt' (place bets) on racehorse meetings that were held in the capital cities of Brisbane, Sydney, and Melbourne.

Several hotels, late Friday afternoon or in the early evening, would provide free 'nibblies' (mostly pastry-based finger food). A *popular* routine amongst the itinerant fraternity began with the 5.00 pm 'seafood raffles' at one of the centrally-located hotels. The lucky patron could win one of several large trays of seafood if one of their purchased tickets was drawn.

The generous-sized seafood tray would consist of two mud crabs, a large red emperor fish, and a one-kilogram bag of prawns (and a six-pack of bottled XXXX beer). Charlie and Chan would win several of these large seafood trays during the season.

At 5.30 pm, the bar staff at this venue would supply patrons with numerous medium-sized trays of finger food. By 6.00 pm, the raffle draws were complete and all of the food had been devoured. A large number of itinerant workers would then relocate to a hotel known colloquially as 'The Zoo' – coined by the local population, who generally regarded this venue as being regularly frequented by a *vast array of wildlife.*

The bar staff at 'The Zoo' would commence providing patrons with trays of finger food around 6.30 pm. Half an hour later and the itinerant collective were on the move once more, to the nearby Clubbers Hotel. The bar staff at this venue would commence bringing out trays of finger food just after 7.00 pm. By 8.00 pm, one had been well and truly fed – no need to buy or cook dinner that night.

For the rest of the evening, the centrally-located hotels would be hubs of boisterous and frivolous activity. At 11.00 pm, these establishments would promptly close. After 11.00 pm, for those that wanted to 'party on' there were only two choices: a nightclub in the Queens Beach region (located several kilometres northeast of central Bowen) or the Operatic Nite Club (four kilometres from the town centre) – but conveniently located about 150 metres from the Edgecombe Village Caravan Park.

One of the centrally-located hotels provided courtesy buses to the Operatic Nite Club between 10.00 pm-11.15 pm. Every Friday night, Charlie and Chan would use one of these fare-free courtesy buses, instead of paying a taxi fare. After they were dropped off at the Operatic Nite Club, they would either continue socialising inside the nightclub or return to the nearby Edgecombe Village Caravan Park.

Inside the Operatic Nite Club, there would be either a band playing or a DJ providing dance music. At 1.00 am, the normal lighting would suddenly illuminate the interior of the venue and the music would cease, tactfully informing all and sundry that the nightly entertainment has come to a sudden halt. The bouncers (nightclub security), politely but forcefully, ensured that all patrons quickly make their way through the exit doors.

Outside, in the fresh tranquil air, patrons could either board a courtesy bus returning to the town centre or use the services of one of several waiting taxis. Residents of Edgecombe Village Caravan Park and El Pedro Caravan Park (now Bowen Palms Caravan Park and a further 500 metres away) simply walked to their destinations.

For some of the residents of the Edgecombe Village Caravan Park, the journey back required the mastery of staggering quietly to their caravan, tent, or motorised home. The ever-vigilant 'garden gnome' (Graham) would be waiting outside the office – sternly eyeing each returning individual – and armed with a waddy/nulla-nulla (an Aboriginal hunting stick). Occasionally, Graham would escort certain individuals to their place of abode. The mismatched combination of an inebriated stupor and the night darkness affected certain people's sense of direction!

Charlie would often assist a heavily intoxicated Chan back to the caravan in an orderly and quiet fashion – but still under the watchful eye of Graham. If a heavily intoxicated Chan was trying to return to the caravan on his own from the nightclub – his sense of direction largely deserted him.

Occasionally, he would wander helplessly back and forth across the highway, unclear on what side of the road the caravan park was located. On one particular night, Chan made his way along a dirt track, on the other side of the highway, and ended up just outside a car-wrecking yard – 'greeted' by two hostile Dobermans. Fortunately for Chan, both dogs were on the other side of the high-wire perimeter!

One Saturday morning, Charlie drove into this particular car-wrecking yard to purchase several spare parts for his vehicle. He was accompanied by Chan. Just after the pair alighted from Charlie's vehicle, the two Dobermans started growling quite *fiercely*. As the owner of the car-wrecking yard casually ambled towards Charlie, the boisterous canines were preoccupied with Chan!

At one point, Chan wanted to put his hand through a sizeable gap in the high-wired fence, to pat them, in a somewhat foolish attempt to *calm* them. He instantly retreated, though, when Lance (the owner of the car-wreck yard) swiftly informed him that 'his boys' would instantly have his hand for a snack!

Charlie then told Lance what spare parts he required for his vehicle. Lance replied, 'No problem.' Gazing at Chan, he remarked with a bemused look, 'You've been here before – haven't you?'

With a deeply puzzled expression, Chan eventually did admit that he *vaguely* remembered two large dogs barking at him – relentlessly in the darkness. Chan further added, that he also hazily remembered hearing a booming faraway voice informing him that the caravan park was on the other side of the highway and about fifty meters further down!

At first, Charlie tried not to laugh as Lance recalled Chan's misdemeanours on this particular night. But he soon conceded defeat. By now, Lance was also laughing quite heartily. Although Chan was smiling, his reddened face was clearly showing a significant level of embarrassment!

By the end of the tomato-picking season, Chan had practically achieved near-celebrity status. His numerous 'exploits' had become well known within the local population and the itinerant collective – especially in connection with the hotel and nightclub scene.

On the nightclub dance floor, Chan's over-the-top passion for dancing soon provided a source of amusement for other twinkle-toed dance floor occupiers. Chan's *Saturday Night Fever* dance moves soon ensured that he would be provided with sizeable dance-floor space – mainly to avoid colliding with other dancing frolickers.

On one particular Thursday night, Chan tried to enter the nightclub section of the Davison Hotel – still in his work attire. Along with noticeably tomato-stained hands and feet, he was also wearing shorts, a singlet, and a pair of thongs (flip-flops). Fonu, the Tongan-born bouncer at the entrance, wouldn't let Chan in. *Closed* footwear needed to be worn. Chan returned to the main bar.

Determined not to be defeated, Chan calmly asked some of the patrons if he could borrow a pair of closed footwear. Unfortunately for Chan, most patrons were wearing thongs! An English backpacker (Paul), though, removed his pair of bright white runners and gave them to Chan; provided that they were returned to him the next evening. One slight problem, however, Paul was about thirty centimetres taller than Chan! Now wearing a pair of runners – several sizes too big – Chan gleefully returned to the entrance of the nightclub. Fonu allowed him to enter – much to the amusement of staff and other patrons.

During the last week in October, employment on the tomato farm came to a sudden halt. Although Charlie was keen to leave the area and venture southwards, Chan informed him that he had obtained a further ten days of employment at another tomato farm. This particular tomato farm was located on Collinsville Road (now the Bowen Development Road), owned by Eddie McMurphy, affectionately known locally as 'Steady Eddie'.

Compared to their previous place of employment, Charlie and Chan soon discovered that this tomato farm seemed to operate mainly in a somewhat haphazard manner. Besides a lack of organised structure in the tomato field (i.e. no paddock boss), luscious weeds were in abundance between the rows of tomatoes. The pair, nevertheless, still managed to earn a substantial amount of money during this period of employment. Equally important though, 'Steady Eddie' was a terrific fellow to work for and in future seasons, Charlie would work on his tomato farm on several occasions.

Eddie was quite a laid-back character, enhanced by an equally calm persona. Both Charlie and Chan enjoyed several light-hearted discussions with him. Initially, Charlie thought that Eddie might have acquired the nickname 'Steady' due to his overall calm nature but he earnt the nickname – due to his driving habits.

Eddie always drove a tray truck. Regardless of where he drove, Eddie tended to drive at *half* the allowable speed limit. For example, within the town of Bowen, where the speed limit was 60 kilometres, he was content to putter along at 30 kilometres per hour. On the highway, where the speed limit was generally 100 km/h, Eddie would casually cruise along at a speed of between 50-60 km/h. With the driver's side window down, he would rest his arm on top of the main part of the door, halfway out of the window – whistling whilst he drove.

Once employment had ceased on Eddie's tomato farm, the tomato-picking season within the region was practically finished. The following day, Charlie and Chan were on the Bruce Highway, heading southwards towards Brisbane. After staying in Brisbane for several days, the pair parted ways. Charlie continued driving along several highways in a mostly southwest direction. After travelling for two days and over 1100 kilometres, he arrived in the New South Wales town of Young: the *Cherry Capital* of Australia.

97

6

Life is Cherry Ripe

On a sunny, near-cloudless afternoon, Charlie drove along the Olympic Way (now known as the Olympic Highway). Five kilometres away from the town of Young, a large colourful billboard greeted him: 'Welcome to Young – The Cherry Capital of Australia'. It was mid-November.

Nestled in the South West Slopes region of New South Wales, Young was named after Sir John Young: governor of NSW from 1861 to 1867. Originally known as Lambing Flat, the town is probably best known for its past goldfields and the 'Lambing Flat riots.' It was renamed Young in 1863. A popular myth that circulated for many years was that Chinese gold prospectors (in the 19th century) had named the area *Yong*.

Before he departed from Bowen (North Queensland), Charlie had been given an address and a telephone number of a cherry orchard in the Young district. Following the handwritten directions, Charlie drove a further two kilometres beyond the large billboard. Upon noticing a large area of cattle yards, he turned right into Mangle Road (immediately before the cattle yards) and proceeded along this road until he came upon Jacuzzi Road. After turning right into Jacuzzi Road, Charlie soon came upon a large sign: 'Loonavale Orchards'.

Charlie drove straight to the entrance of the packing shed. A short time later, he was greeted by Marcus (one of the orchard's managers). Charlie would soon learn that Marcus was one-sixth of the management team. The six orchard managers all had equal shares in the company but the owner, who Charlie would only meet once, still had the majority of shares. Two years later, the owner (Antonio) would relinquish his shares and the management team would have sole ownership and total control of the company.

Although Charlie would eventually meet all the company managers, he mostly dealt with Marcus. After a brief chat, Marcus directed him to the tenting area of the campsite, located near the packing shed. Charlie soon had his tent pitched up on a powered site. The campsite, comprising of caravans (mainly) and tents, was nearly at full capacity.

Marcus then casually informed Charlie that the start of the main cherry-picking season was still several days away. In the meantime, there was a different type of employment: picking snow peas for the next three days, but only for several hours each morning.

The campsite (one of three orchard campsites) would be home for Charlie for the next few weeks. Most of the itinerant workers were residing in caravans and largely distanced themselves from the tent community. The large amenities block effectively separated the two groups of fruit pickers. Charlie would rarely speak to the caravan dwellers, largely regarding them as being 'cliquey' and unsociable towards the tent dwellers.

Within the confines of the tent community, Charlie would regularly chat with his next-door neighbours. His neighbours were four former female school friends from metropolitan Sydney. They shared a large tent that contained several rooms. It soon became apparent to Charlie that the four young ladies (Daisy, Cindy, Mandy, and Florence), aged in their early twenties, were basically in the area for the 'experience'. During the cherry-picking season, they would work together as one team.

The next morning, Charlie walked to a small field (containing the snow pea crop), near the campsite. A small group of people had also arrived. The majority of the campsite residents, however, had decided to wait for the onset of the cherry-picking season. Charlie's next-door neighbours were still fast asleep as he walked past their tent.

The snow pea picking commenced just after 7.00 am. By 11.00 am, selected rows of ripened snow peas had been completely harvested. Charlie soon realised why most of the camp dwellers had chosen not to engage in any snow pea picking. For a start, this type of work was back-breaking. Even worse, from a financial perspective, this employment venture was barely profitable. As the hotel establishments in Young commenced trading hours at 11.00 am, Charlie was soon on his way into town. The snow pea picking venture, for these several days, primarily provided Charlie with 'beer'' money!

During the six-week cherry-picking season, Charlie largely regarded life on the orchard, outside work hours, as being quite dull. Instead, he opted to patronise several of Young's licensed premises on an almost daily basis: in particular, the Commercial Hotel or the Young Services Club.

Several of the management team from Loonavale Orchards were regular patrons at the Commercial hotel. Charlie, generally, would only converse with Marcus. As he resided in one of the upstairs rooms, Marcus would be in the downstairs lounge area every evening. Charlie would occasionally purchase dinner in this hotel (Marcus dined there every night) but his favourite eating place was the sole Chinese Restaurant in Young: The Wok and Roll.

Once the cherry-picking season commenced, one needed to wander to the packing shed every morning to view a large blackboard that detailed what the 'work situation' was for that particular working day. Each morning, around 5.45 am, Marcus would write on the blackboard: the starting time; the location (i.e. the orchard block number); and, whether it was a workday or a day of rest.

Charlie would emerge from his tent each morning by 6.00 am. Somewhat sheepishly, he would wander to the packing shed to view the blackboard. As Charlie returned to his tent, passing his next-door neighbours, one of the half-awoken ladies would poke her head through the tent entrance and ask Charlie what the daily work plan was!

During the cherry-picking season, the early-morning antics of these four young ladies could be best described as amusing. Charlie quickly sensed that they relished any late starts or days off. They would generally emerge from the large tent at the same time. Then, they would all casually amble towards the amenities block.

After spending considerable time in the female restroom, they all re-emerged in nice clean clothes, their hair was well brushed and makeup had been freshly applied. Additionally, they had applied fresh nail polish: each young lady had their own 'style' and colour.

In stark contrast, the typical itinerant worker would generally wear well-worn, fruit-stained clothing purchased mainly from Op-Shops (opportunity shops). Long-sleeved, light-coloured, thin cotton shirts (originally business shirts) were a favourite. Hair grooming and shaving were practically non-existent during the fruit-picking season.

Throughout the cherry-picking season, Charlie would work near the young ladies on many occasions. He soon realised that his daily tally of lugs (plastic rectangular-shaped baskets), filled with cherries, was the same amount (or even more) than the combined tally of the young foursome!

The young lasses took frequent rest breaks and showed little interest in earning a substantial income. Throughout the day, they would eat plenty of cherries and in an attempt to combat the boredom of cherry-picking, would occasionally engage in playful bouts of throwing cherries at each other. Meanwhile, Charlie's work ethic was to provide a source of amusement for the ladies. Instead of actual rest breaks, he would only stop for the occasional quick sip of water. Twice a day, Charlie would eat a sandwich with one hand and continued picking cherries with the other hand!

During the second week of the cherry-picking season, the tenting section of the campsite was to have a new resident: Les. His accommodation was a multi-dented (and rusted) light-blue 1968 Holden HK Premier Sedan. Les parked his vehicle on the other side of the ladies' large tent. It didn't take long for the ladies to be greatly unsettled by Les' *creepiness.*

Charlie deemed Les as a potential social misfit - practically from his first verbal encounter with him. Early in the conversation piece, Les 'reminisced' his time in juvenile detention centres and further added that he had also spent a sizeable portion of his adult life in and out of the penal system! He had been released from Bathurst Gaol (now Bathurst Correctional Complex) just two months earlier.

Charlie soon regarded Les as a persistent 'utterer of fabrications' (a compulsive liar), but even worse, he had woefully inappropriate views on women. As a result, Les was widely despised within the whole campsite – especially by his four female next-door neighbours. On the third day, the ladies complained to the management team concerning Les' blatant unacceptable behaviour.

During the late afternoon of the fourth day, the *entire* management team walked into the tenting area and approached him. Les was given his pay packet and ordered to vacate the campsite immediately. After delivering a barrage of verbal abuse and death threats, he slowly drove through the campsite and onto the public roadway. Eighteen months later, Charlie spotted Les' car, several times, in Bowen (1943 kilometres from Young). Fortunately, though, he would successfully avoid crossing paths with him!

As the end of the cherry-picking season approached, Charlie had managed to save a substantial amount of money. With 10-12 days remaining in the season, Charlie learnt that the cherry-picking season in the Orange district (180 kilometres from Young) was about to commence.

Throughout the season, Loonavale Orchards had a 'bonus' system in place for each cherry picker. They would, supposedly, pay an extra dollar for each full lug of cherries picked during the season – but only if you stayed to the end of the cherry-picking season. In other words, one needed to stay until the last day to be paid the bonus. This so-called bonus system was primarily a scam. The word bonus should have been substituted with the word *bogus.*

Primarily, the ingenious plan was to discourage the itinerant worker from moving to Orange for the start of their main cherry-picking season. The two cherry-picking seasons often overlapped for a period of between one and two weeks. An itinerant's earning capacity during these two weeks was generally much higher within the Orange area. The last two weeks of the Young cherry-picking season, on the other hand, could be quite sporadic – several days off, along with half-day or part-day employment.

Charlie tried to have his bonus paid out to him but in response, Marcus declared, 'The management team will only authorise the payout of a bonus on the very last day of the cherry-picking season.' Externally, Charlie grudgingly accepted this scenario. Internally, he was livid – but Charlie had a plan.

Early one Saturday morning, Charlie calmly wandered into the deserted packing shed. He gathered twenty unused cherry cartons and casually strolled back to his tent. The previous day, Charlie had filled his large esky with cherries (with two ice packs on top). Inside the tent, Charlie quickly packed the cherries into the empty cartons!

A short time later, Charlie dismantled his tent and quickly packed everything into his vehicle. Next, he discreetly drove out of the campsite and onto Jacuzzi Road. Before reaching his intended destination (the small town of Lucknow, ten kilometres from Orange), Charlie decided to stop at a rest area, just outside the town of Cowra (71km from Young and 92km from Orange).

Just before the entrance to the rest area, Charlie attached a large cardboard sign to a road post that read CHERRIES FOR SALE. Two hours later, he had sold all twenty cartons of cherries. Selling at ten dollars a carton, Charlie's 'bonus' amounted to $200!

Charlie arrived in the small town of Lucknow in the mid-afternoon and headed straight for the lone tavern. A short time later, he was enjoying a refreshing cold beverage. Not much had changed since the last time Charlie was there. Spud and Jed were sitting on their favourite bar stools, merrily downing one schooner after another. Publican Norm was still grumpy. One major detail, however, soon caught Charlie's eye!

The menu, written in white chalk on a blackboard, had *significantly* changed. No more hamburgers, hot chips, hot dogs, sandwiches, etc. Only two options remained: pies and sausage rolls. Jed soon informed Charlie that Gladys (Norm's wife) had recently separated from him and added that Norm's 'cooking skills' were solely limited to the use of a microwave!

Three hours later, Charlie drove to Kevin and Allan's orchard and he was soon chatting amicably with Kevin. After a brief discussion, Charlie moved his belongings into the accommodation quarters (inside the packing shed). This would be his abode of residence for the duration of the upcoming cherry-picking season, commencing in two days.

On the first day, just after 6.00 am, Charlie (along with several others) was in the orchard block that contained the cherry trees. Unlike the apple, pear, and stone-fruit trees, the cherry trees were *huge*. They were decades old but they had been properly pruned.

At Loonavale Orchards, Charlie only needed to use an aluminium six-rung ladder, when he couldn't reach the cherries whilst standing on the ground. In stark contrast, all the ladders provided in this cherry block were either ten-rung or twelve-rung ladders. Solely made of steel, they were quite heavy and awkward to carry.

The early morning 'eager-beavers' were soon assigned to the cherry trees that were ready to be harvested/picked, as indicated by several bright red ribbons tied to the branches. After being assigned to a cherry tree, Charlie grabbed one of the twelve-rung ladders. On the ground, a dozen empty metal tins (old recycled half-sized honey tins) had been placed near the trunk of the tree. Despite the size of the cherry tree, Charlie soon discovered that he could still fill the empty tins with cherries at quite a brisk rate.

Whilst working on Loonavale Orchards, Charlie had acquired several *tricks*:

> 1. To let his thumbnails grow longer and use them to cut (easily) the bunch of cherries;
> 2. To tuck a branch under an arm to pick cherries quickly with both hands at once;
> 3. To place the ladder in the 'correct' position each time as he shuffled around a cherry tree.

Over the next two hours, more people had arrived at the orchard – seventy to eighty in total. As the cherry-picking work was paid at piece-rate, instead of an hourly rate, there was no set start or finish times. Kevin and Allan, however, did have one rule: the earliest start time was 6.00 am and the latest finishing time was 5.00 pm.

Each morning, Spud was also one of the early starters, despite being severely hung-over. His work routine, generally, was the same each working day. From 6.00 am to 9.00 am, he would work quite quickly, filling a substantial number of metal tins with cherries. Just after 9.00 am, Spud would commence his daily 'thermos and bickies' routine.

Spud, firstly, would pour himself a large mug of black tea. Over the next several minutes, he'd consume several biscuits. Then, Spud would casually go for a stroll (with the mug of tea in one hand) within the cherry block. For the next half hour or so, he would constantly greet people, offering *positive moral support* in an endeavour to motivate and brighten someone's day!

Eventually, Spud would return and recommence cherry-picking. For the next several hours, he would casually toil away – at a noticeably slower pace than the early morning session. Around 1.00 pm, Spud would stop and pour himself another mug of black tea. With mug in hand, he would again go for another stroll in amongst the cherry trees, chatting to numerous people. Half an hour later, Spud would be making his way out of the orchard – heading directly to the tavern.

For about two weeks, the main part of the cherry-picking season coincided with the commencement of a long school-holiday period, before Christmas Eve and finishing either at the end of December or within the first week of January. This meant that large numbers of local school-aged teenagers/children would be in the orchards trying to earn some money for Christmas presents and family holidays.

Small groups of teenagers tended to work together on the same large cherry tree but most of them would still keep their tallies separate from each other. Additionally, family groups, especially mums with their offspring, would also work on the one large cherry tree. Rivalry and petty quarrelling – especially amongst the family groups – persisted throughout the day, best described as quite 'entertaining' at times. One such notorious family group consisted of 'Ma Baker' and her brood of seven, ranging in ages from eight to eighteen.

Although this clan of eight would work together on the same large tree, they largely kept their tallies separate. Ma Baker, though, would distribute her tins of cherries equally amongst her offspring. The group would generally toil away each day between the hours of 7.00 am and 4.00 pm.

During each working day, Ma Baker would be regularly screaming and yelling at her offspring, especially the younger ones, emphasising that they needed to keep their 'minds on the job'. She would organise her 'clan' accordingly; the older siblings were assigned with the ladder duties, whilst the younger siblings were to pick the lower hanging cherries. Ma Baker tended to pick the cherries in the high-middle sections of the tree, working mainly off a twelve-rung ladder. Occasionally she would have one foot on a ladder rung and the other foot on a large branch, enabling her to pick cherries with both hands at once.

At some point during the day, mainly in the afternoon, the younger siblings would occasionally attempt to engage in clandestine-like cherry-throwing warfare. Ma Baker's 'sixth sense' would swiftly intervene and *a barrage of hysterics* would immediately follow. If any of the youngsters turned on the 'waterworks' (crying), she would swiftly descend the ladder. Her principal mode of discipline was a mild slap on the offending child's face and the crying would cease immediately!

Another family group working together on this orchard was the notorious Woodstock family. Though they largely kept to themselves, other cherry-pickers tended to shun them anyway, largely deeming their general behaviour as *weird*. The group consisted of twelve members but they divided themselves into two working groups of six. They would pick cherries on two separate trees, but next to each other. Each group comprised two adults and four children: Ringo and Rosie were the adults in one group whilst Rocky and Mary-May were the adults in the other group.

It soon became apparent that the majority of the cherry-pickers did not want to work near the Bakers or the Woodstocks. Kevin and his son Rob regularly received requests to be placed out of 'earshot' from these two family groups! The Baker clan, especially Ma Baker, were quite a noisy lot. The joyous extended Woodstock family, on the other hand, annoyed the other cherry-pickers for another reason – incessant Christmas carol singing.

Charlie detested Christmas carol singing as it reminded him of unpleasant childhood memories. To combat this irksome noise, he would increase the volume on his radio transistor (several levels) in an attempt to neutralise the 'asynchronous whining'.

Around noon each day, the Woodstocks would cease work and commence a one-hour luncheon break. Before any consumption of food, they would firstly sit on the ground, in a circle, under the shade of a large cherry tree. Holding hands with the person on either side of them, they then recited a mantra thanking the Mighty Lord for the meal that they were about to receive – a choice between vegemite, peanut butter, or pickled sandwiches.

Upon the consumption of all the sandwiches, the group commenced singing old-fashioned children's songs such as "Ring a Ring o' Roses", "Frere Jacques" and "Here We Go Round the Mulberry Bush" – dreadfully and annoyingly. Charlie began to think that this spectacle was maybe some form of *ritualistic gratefulness*: a means of preparedness to slave tirelessly but purposefully during the next few hours of cherry-picking perhaps?

Charlie soon learnt that Spud had known the Woodstocks for quite a long time – and he didn't like them. Spud informed Charlie of several aspects of their oddball behaviour.

According to Spud, one such aspect of their oddball behaviour involved an even larger group of this family (fifteen or more). They would gather several times a week, in the evening, at one of Orange's park reserves. In a conga-line formation, they would commence jogging! This bizarre ritual occurred all year round – even during the bitterly cold winter months.

As in Young's recent cherry-picking season, Charlie continued his practice of not stopping for meal breaks. Whilst devouring a sandwich, he would continue to pick cherries with the other hand. Charlie, though, opted not to indulge in this type of work practice whilst working on a twelve-rung ladder, purely as a means of common sense – not as a means to adhering to any 'health and safety' measures. *Health and Safety Regulations*, practically, were non-existent on orchards or vegetable farms at the time!

On one particular day, Charlie was working next to a group of four middle-aged males and wondered to himself whether they might have met at an *Alcoholics Anonymous* meeting or not. Before the commencement of cherry-picking, the four of them each had a cigarette and a can of beer! During the working day, they would have regular 'ciggy and beer' breaks but did consume food during their long luncheon break.

During the luncheon break, the group was quite bemused with Charlie's practice of eating a sandwich with one hand and picking cherries with the other. One of them even suggested to Charlie that he should sit down and have a proper break. A mildly-bewildered Charlie quickly reminded the group that they were being paid by the volume of cherries picked (i.e. by piece rate) – not by an hourly rate.

A few minutes before 5.00 pm, Charlie filled up his last tin of cherries just before this group had filled their last one. A short time later, the last tins of cherries were collected and weighed. Rob informed the group that they had collectively picked a total of forty-seven tins of cherries for the day. Cheekily, Charlie asked Rob what his final tally was for the day (even though he already knew). Rob replied with a wry smile, 'Forty-five tins today… well done Charlie.' A sullen silence from the foursome instantly filled the air!

A vital aspect of the cherry-picking season was the intriguing process of weighing *every* tin of cherries. Each day, three or four people were required to pick up every tin of cherries. Next, they would weigh each tin of cherries using imperial-measuring scales.

Writing on pieces of foolscap paper (attached to a clipboard), they would record the weight of each tin of cherries picked by an individual or group of cherry pickers. Once weighed and recorded, the cherries were then emptied into small wooden bins which were on bin trailers attached to a tractor.

The empty metal tins were returned to the cherry pickers. This group of employees was paid a flat daily rate; their hours were usually from 7.00 am to 5.00 pm.

At the time, cherry pickers on this orchard were paid 20c per imperial pound of cherries picked. Each working day, Charlie would generally pick between 500–600 pounds of cherries; earning $100-$120 per day. The majority of cherry growers (in the Orange district), however, paid 40-45 cents per kilogram of cherries picked.

[Note: 1 kilogram equates to about 2.2 pounds in weight].

A common problem with this method of payment (being paid by weight) was that some varieties of cherries were notably heavier than others. Eventually, the 'honey half-tins' were replaced with plastic fruit crates (lugs). The lugs were filled with cherries to 'water-level' and, subsequently, cherry-pickers were paid per how many lugs they had picked for the day.

At that particular time, the main cherry-picking season would generally only last for 2-3 weeks. In future cherry-picking seasons, though, more varieties of cherries would be planted and harvested. Many years later, a typical cherry-picking season in the Orange region would extend from five to seven weeks (although the main crop may only last for 3-4 weeks).

As there was a gap of five weeks between the cherry-picking season and the stone-fruit picking season, Charlie decided to relocate to another region. After departing from the Orange region, he travelled along The Escort Way to the town of Forbes. After Forbes, Charlie travelled along the Newell Highway to the New South Wales/Victoria border. After a seven-hour journey and a road distance of 598 kilometres, he arrived in the Victorian city of Shepparton.

7

South of the Rio Murray

After a seven-hour drive, Charlie was in the small town of Ratatutra, located in central Victoria. Whilst having a cool refreshing beverage in one of the town's hotel establishments, he crossed paths with a fellow seasonal itinerant worker: Jeff. Charlie had worked with him during the tomato-picking season in Bowen (North Queensland) a few months prior. Although employment opportunities appeared to be limited, Jeff assured Charlie that they will be both working within the next couple of days. It was the third week in January.

Several beers later, the pair left the hotel. After walking a mere twenty metres, they stood outside a 'private' café. Above the doorway, Charlie espied an old and barely-readable sign, *Café Ma Freer*. Attached to the inside of one of the glass panes (of the large front window) read a more recent sign: The Calabrian Social Club.

A cheerful Jeff went through the open doorway. Charlie followed hesitantly. Inside the private café, there was a mixture of middle-aged and elderly males who were either tomato growers or retired tomato growers. Jeff was welcomed with open arms as he had worked for many of these gentlemen over numerous past tomato-picking seasons. In stark contrast, Charlie was mostly met with cold death stares – and the playing of the *Godfather* theme as background music in the café only added to his general feeling of uneasiness.

After Jeff was widely greeted by the café's patrons, he was soon discussing employment prospects with two brothers: Giuseppe and Alphonse. A subdued Charlie stood behind Jeff.

Whilst Alphonse was relatively passive, Giuseppe, on the other hand, was quite lively and animated; freely (and wildly) gesticulating with both hands, along with seemingly unnecessary and ridiculous contorted facial expressions!

Ten minutes later, both Jeff and Charlie were informed that they could commence employment at Giuseppe and Alphonse's tomato farm, located near the town of Munchonit, the next morning.

In the early evening, Charlie pitched his tent in the camping area of a caravan park: two kilometres from Ratatutra. An hour later, he cooked himself a hearty meat-based meal on the communal barbeque in the camp kitchen. For the rest of the evening, Charlie drank several glasses of muscat fortified wine. He slept well that night.

Just before 6.00 am the next morning, Jeff and Charlie waited patiently at the entrance of a tomato field, along with

80+ other aspiring tomato pickers. A few minutes later, Charlie was frantically spraying himself (mainly face, neck and hands) with insect repellent. Even at that time in the morning, the relentless swarms of flies were merciless – seemingly on a mission to annoy humans – to a point well past an acceptable level of insanity.

Eventually, the tomato picking commenced. Charlie would work alone. He was directed by Alphonse to a block of tomatoes (15 metres by 40 metres) that consisted of ten rows of tomato vines.

Charlie was given twenty empty buckets. Once all the buckets were filled with ripened (or near-ripened) tomatoes, he would then empty them into a nearby wooden bin. Charlie's daily earnings were based on the number of these bins filled. At the time, the piece rate per full bin of tomatoes was $40. He would fill two or three bins each working day.

The majority of tomato pickers tended to work in groups. Only a handful of itinerant fruit-pickers, such as Jeff and Charlie, worked alone. Many of these groups were family units. These family units (of a particular ethnicity) would travel up from Melbourne every January for the tomato-picking season. Mainly residing in caravan parks, within a thirty-kilometre radius of the tomato farm, they would toil in the tomato fields for three to four months each year.

Charlie would later learn that the vast majority of these family groups were either on a Newstart Allowance (unemployment benefits) or a Disability Support Pension (invalid pension) – all year-round. Within the itinerant tomato-picking community, the invalid pension was often referred to as the *Back Pension*. One major advantage of the 'back pension' was that the Disability Support Pension form only had to be handed into a Centrelink office once every three months. The Newstart Allowance form, in contrast, had to be handed in (to a Centrelink office) every two weeks.

Each day would be marred with what Charlie soon coined as *organised chaos*. The largely unpleasant working environment was a combination of the following: layers of dust would be constantly wafting through the air; an ever-present 'buzz' of activity (i.e. largely undesirable noise levels); and, the ever-persistent swarms of flies. On the second day of tomato-picking, Charlie attached protective netting to his straw hat which covered the face and part of his neck. But as the commencement of the pear-picking season was nearing, he decided to quit this line of employment after just one week.

Two days after leaving the tomato farm, Charlie casually drove through the Ardmona locality (ten kilometres west of the city of Shepparton) seeking pear-picking opportunities. He soon came upon a pear orchard with a large sign, next to the main entrance: Pride of Sicilia Orchards. Underneath this sign was a smaller one, *Pear Pickers Wanted.*

After a brief discussion with the pear orchard owner (Angelo), Charlie drove back to the caravan park and quickly packed up his camping equipment. When he returned to the pear orchard, he moved into a room that was part of an old building complex. The room contained only three pieces of furniture: a bed frame; a well-used mattress; and, an 'antique' wardrobe. The floor, the walls, and the ceiling were all constructed of concrete – a 'cement doggy box' (as described in chapter one). The room, however, did have a power socket. This meant that Charlie could have his portable fan running – an essential aid for sleeping during a warm summer night.

During a good part of the day, these 'cement doggie boxes' could be best described as large *ovens*; especially when the temperatures exceeded forty degrees Celsius (or 104 degrees Fahrenheit). Fortunately, close to the living quarter's block, there was a small hut. The hut contained a communal kitchen and an adjoining lounge room. In the lounge area, there was an old air conditioner – but it worked exceptionally well.

Early the next morning, bleary-eyed pear-pickers gathered outside the small hut. Eventually, the distinct sound of a rapidly-approaching quad bike could be heard. Just after greeting all and sundry, Angelo casually announced to them that they would be *size picking* the pears for the next few days. Everyone was given a metal measuring ring. The only pears that were to be picked were the ones that couldn't pass through the ring. Unfortunately, the majority of the pears on the trees would be undersized!

Over the next several days, Charlie would only pick two bins of pears each day. Along with other pear-pickers, he would cease pear-picking by 1.00 pm. The afternoons would either be spent in the air-conditioned comfort of the hut's communal area or one of the air-conditioned hotels in the nearby town of Mooroopna.

Similar to previous communal-living experiences, Charlie would yet again meet quite a few intriguing characters! Firstly, there were the two Italian-born gentlemen, aged in their early sixties, who consistently wore attire reminiscent of 'Sunday church' clothing of a bygone era: trousers held up with belts/suspenders; old-style 'dressy' long-sleeved shirts; and, well-worn 1950s-style footwear.

Each working day, the pair was back in the air-conditioned hut by midday. They would spend the whole afternoon drinking homemade wine, poured from ageless recyclable wine flagons into ceramic mugs. They would constantly mutter quietly to each other in Italian, albeit with an increased level of slurring as they consumed each mug of wine.

Then there was Fijian-born Tommy. Aged in his fifties, his greying hairstyle had an uncanny resemblance to that of Don King (a former boxing promoter). Tommy would only work every second day and would remind his fellow residing pear pickers, 'Work one day … recover the next!'

Lastly, there were several middle-aged Serbians/Croatians (commonly known as *Yugos* or *Jugs* at the time). Although they toiled quite well in the orchard, they tended to be socially inebriated for most of the day! Their early morning (5.30 am-6.00 am) 'ritual' would commence with a cold beer and a cigarette. Around 10.00 am, they would gather together for a 'beer and ciggy' break.

After finishing work for the day, they would even have a beer whilst showering! Then, they would all then venture into the nearby town of Mooroopna and patronise a particular hotel – commonly known, within the itinerant community, as the *Jumanji Pub*. By 9.00 pm, they had all returned to the orchard residence.

Within the confines of the orchard, conversations between the Croats/Serbs tended to be quite boisterous, bordering on the point of being obnoxiously comical at times. Somewhat surprisingly though, they got on quite well with each other. In future travels, Charlie would occasionally encounter an aura of flared tensions between individuals or groups that would specifically identify themselves as being either a diehard Croatian or a diehard Serbian. The result: heated arguments or severe physical altercations (or both) between these two groups!

After seven days of slow progression, Charlie decided to seek employment at another orchard in the Ardmona area. As he drove around the area, Charlie noticed that practically all of the orchards contained large (and old) trees. Even worse, they were poorly pruned. Many orchards even had whole blocks of pear trees which could be best described as being *squared-shape*. The tops and sides of the trees had been lopped off via the use of chainsaws; the interior branches and limbs were virtually untouched. He decided to seek pear-picking employment outside the Ardmona area.

After driving through the city of Shepparton, Charlie continued eastwards towards the small town of Shepparton East. Whilst in the eastern outskirts of Shepparton, he decided to call into The Underhander Hotel. The hotel was a popular drinking hole for itinerant pear pickers in the Shepparton East region.

Upon entering the premises, Charlie soon recognised quite a few familiar faces! He immediately began conversing with one of the veteran itinerant fruit pickers (Dan). Dan was more commonly known within the itinerant network as 'Pluto'. He suggested to Charlie that the Pine Lodge Caravan Park (now known as *Secura Lifestyle Shepparton East Holiday Park*) was a valuable source of information regarding pear-picking opportunities within the Shepparton East region.

Dan further stated that the owner of the Pine Lodge Caravan Park would have a list of pear growers, within the Shepparton East region, who were actively seeking employees for the upcoming pear-picking season.

Two hours later, Charlie was in the caravan park office discussing accommodation availability and the upcoming pear-picking season with the manager: Donald. He stated to Charlie that pear picking within the Shepparton East region would commence within the next two or three days. Charlie informed Donald that he would return to the caravan park within an hour.

Charlie immediately headed back to Angelo's orchard to collect his gear – and his earnings. As a 'doleful' Angelo handed Charlie his paycheque, he inquired into the sudden departure. Before Charlie could even respond, Angelo stated sarcastically to him that he was making 'good' money on his orchard. Charlie swiftly retorted, 'Earning $400 in seven days … less than $60 a day … is about half the amount I usually earn!'

A now-bewildered Angelo sternly ordered him to be off his orchard within half an hour. With a broad smirk, Charlie calmly replied, 'Don't worry … I'll be gone in less than ten minutes.'

After Charlie had pitched his tent and paid the weekly site fee, Donald gave him a list of orchards that were seeking pear-picking personnel. As it was now late afternoon,

Charlie decided to leave the job hunting until the next morning. During the evening, Charlie would meet most of the tent-dwelling residents either in the outdoor cooking/barbeque area or in the large indoor communal room.

Pine Lodge Caravan Park would be home for Charlie for the next five weeks. During this time, he would engage in a high level of rapport with his fellow tent-dwellers: a mixture of foreign backpackers, novice fruit-pickers, and experienced itinerant workers. During the upcoming pear picking season and despite working 9-11 hours nearly every day, Charlie's social life thrived.

The tenting community was, in general, quite a friendly lot. Outside work hours, Charlie would regularly engage in daily light-hearted conversations with them. Pear picking, though, was rarely discussed!

Every Friday afternoon, Charlie would venture to the Underhander Hotel, taking advantage of the 'Happy Hour' (5.30-6.30 pm). All drinks were half-priced. The hotel was packed with both itinerant workers and local regulars. During Happy Hour, it was quite common for tables to be covered with jugs of beer! It would take a couple of hours for these jugs of beer to be consumed. By 9.00 pm, however, most of the itinerant workers had already left the hotel establishment as they needed to rise early the next morning.

The next morning, Charlie sought out his next place of pear-picking employment. After driving along several roads in the Shepparton East region and checking out several orchards, he eventually came upon one that contained blocks of small to medium-sized pear trees. The pear orchard appeared to be a relatively new one.

After driving past the orchard, a large Mediterranean-styled homestead loomed into view. An unpaved roadway, close to the homestead, led directly to a small packing shed. Charlie alighted from his vehicle and walked towards the entrance of the packing shed. A short, stockily-built, and balding gentleman soon emerged and introduced himself as Jimmy.

Charlie politely asked Jimmy (a Greek-born Australian) if he was still seeking pear-pickers. He, firstly, asked Charlie if he had any previous fruit-picking experience.

Charlie replied, 'Yes!'

'Ok, we'll be starting in two days.'

Jimmy continued, 'I only need three pear-pickers. I already have two, Alain and Ahmed... you'll be the third one.'

A chatty Jimmy continued talking to Charlie for the next ten minutes, revealing that he and his family had relocated to Shepparton East from Melbourne some ten years prior. Jimmy further divulged, proudly, how he had built the orchard from scratch.

For the next five weeks, Charlie would tirelessly toil away each day for 9-11 hours. An exception, though, was a four-day gap between the two varieties of pears grown on this orchard: Williams (also known as Williams' bon chrétien pear or Bartlett pear) and the Packhams (also known as Packham's Triumph).

On a warm but tranquil morning, Charlie arrived at the orchard just after 6.00 am. He had arrived with French-born Alain, who also resided in the camping area of the Pine Lodge Caravan Park. The third pear-picker, Ahmed, arrived a few minutes later. Jimmy soon emerged, with a large mug of coffee in one hand. A short time later, three 'ageless' Massey Ferguson tractors gently roared down a narrow dirt path towards the first block of pear trees to be picked.

Throughout this five-week pear season, Alain and Charlie (individually) would fill 8-10 bins of pears each working day. Ahmed, on the other hand, would generally pick 6-7 bins a day.

Although Charlie would occasionally converse with Alain, he would rarely speak to the quietly-spoken Ahmed. Charlie, however, soon learnt (from Jimmy) that Ahmed was aged in his early thirties and married with five young children. The pear-picking was Ahmed's *secondary* means of employment. His main source of income was driving a taxi in the evening/night; five or six days per week.

As Alain did not possess a vehicle, he would travel with Charlie each day to and from the orchard. Charlie later learned that Alain was an Australian citizen via a previous marriage to an Australian woman; he had also been divorced for just over six years. Inside the caravan park, Charlie would have several long-winded discussions with him. But he soon grew tired of listening to Alain's somewhat bizarre philosophical views on life! After just one week, Charlie began to limit any discussions with him – especially ones that tended to focus on any *meaning of life* concepts.

Alain would regularly draw numerous pencilled sketches of 'brainstorming' diagrams which included buzzwords, a variety of emoticons, and philosophical statements. In the evenings, he would present these sketches to Charlie (and others), either within the camping area or in the communal common room, in an attempt to invoke a serious thought-provoking discussion. Soon, a nonchalant Charlie would casually respond to Alain's sketches with a regular utterance of one word: 'Interesting!'

After about two weeks, Alain realised that Charlie barely showed any interest in his philosophical views. Undeterred, he would still approach individuals/groups (especially in the communal area) in an attempt to instigate non-invasive and light-hearted conversations – and the pencilled sketched diagrams soon emerged. His initial light-hearted conversational tone soon evolved into one of a more serious nature.

Much to Alain's dismay, his theories on the 'meaning of life' were quickly dismissed and the would-be audience would revert, once more, to conversations of a more light-hearted nature. From time to time, Charlie reminded him that *life is fun*, further suggesting to Alain that he should adopt a more positive attitude towards life.

One Friday afternoon, the pear-picking season on Jimmy's orchard came to a halt. The following day, the three pear-pickers joined Jimmy and his extended family for an end-of-season barbeque. The barbeque was, essentially, a 'food fest': several barbequed types of meat (lamb, beef, duck, and chicken); various salads and types of bread/buns; and, a wide choice of desserts.

Jimmy's family was quite pleasant and friendly and the culinary extravaganza was enjoyed by all – even Alain, who was more upbeat than normal. At one point, though, Charlie did overhear Jimmy saying to Alain, 'Life is meant to be enjoyed!'

Two days later, Charlie and Alain left the caravan park. Driving easterly, along the Midland Highway, Charlie passed through the small city of Benalla and continued along the Hume Highway (now the Hume Freeway). At the border city of Albury (in New South Wales), he dropped Alain off at a local bus stop, not far from the freeway. It was the last time that Charlie ever saw him again.

Charlie continued his journey along the Hume Highway for several more hours, before turning onto the Lachlan Valley Way. He continued along this road to the town of Cowra. After driving through Cowra, Charlie then drove along the Mid Western Highway until he reached the town of Blayney. From there, he drove along Millthorpe Road which linked up with the Mitchell Highway. After driving along the Mitchell Highway for several kilometres, Charlie was back in a familiar place – Lucknow's lone tavern.

8

Apples in Orange

Upon arriving in the small town of Lucknow, Charlie headed straight to the lone tavern. As soon as he entered the licensed premises, Charlie was greeted by Jed and Spud, still 'superglued' to their favourite stools, with the encouraging words: 'Back again!'

The only other occupant of the tavern was Norm – the cheerless publican. Sitting at a table several metres away from the bar area, he was deeply engrossed in a newspaper crossword puzzle. Charlie stood patiently at the bar waiting to be served and waited – and waited. Norm was still totally preoccupied with the crossword puzzle. Providing service to a thirsty patron seemed to be a secondary priority for him!

After a couple of minutes, Jed (abhorred by Norm's lack of barman etiquette) alighted from his stool. As he made his way towards the other side of the bar, Jed calmly announced, 'Don't worry Charlie – I'll pour you a beer.'

As if he had been hit by a sudden bolt of lightning, Norm suddenly sprang up from his chair. Brushing Jed aside, he poured a beer for Charlie. Returning to his stool, Jed revealed to Charlie that he had recently completed an RSA (Responsible Serving of Alcohol) certificate.

Jed further admitted that he had poured himself a beer on several occasions over the past two weeks, particularly when Norm was out of sight or just plain lazy to alight from a comfortable chair – engrossed in a crossword or word puzzle. Jed regarded this practice of self-service as *work experience.*

As the late afternoon rolled into the early evening, Charlie noticed on the menu board, a third option to pies and sausage rolls – microwavable chicken rolls. A few minutes later, he was happily devouring one of these chicken rolls. With an element of controlled sarcasm, Charlie 'complimented' Norm on his microwaving skills. Still feeling quite peckish, he politely ordered another chicken roll. An hour later, Charlie was once more making himself at home in the living quarters of the packing shed on Kevin and Alan's orchard.

The next morning, Charlie waited outside the packing shed in readiness for the commencement of another apple-picking season. After briefly chatting with Kevin, he was soon reunited with the previous year's apple-picking crew: Jed, Tom, Bill, and Ben.

Before the first apple had been picked, Charlie had already made it his goal to fill a minimum of eight bins of apples each day. Commencing work around 7.00 am, he would consistently accomplish this feat by 5.00 pm. During the season, Charlie often worked beside Jed, who would also aim to fill eight bins of apples each day. The pair would regularly race against each other but Jed was always quicker! After driving the tractor (with full bins of apples) back to the packing shed, Jed would drive straight to the tavern.

Jed's daily work ethic involved quite an interesting strategy. After each full bin, he would open a cold can of beer and have a five-minute break. After several long sips, Jed would commence filling his next bin, finishing the rest of the can as he worked. He rarely drank any water!

After Charlie had driven his tractor back to the packing shed, he too would drive straight to the tavern. A freshly-poured schooner (425ml) of Tooheys *Hunter Old*, purchased by Jed, was waiting for him on the bar counter!

Similar to the previous apple-picking season, there were periods of no employment in Kevin and Alan's orchard. There was a two-week gap between the last of the red apple varieties and the start of the Granny Smith apple picking season. Charlie, however, would secure employment at a neighbouring orchard. The orchardist, Paolo, had contacted Kevin and stated to him that he required three people for seven or eight days of apple-picking.

As Paolo only had two tractors, Kevin lent Charlie one of his ageless Massey Ferguson's. Even though Paolo's orchard backed onto a section of Kevin and Alan's orchard, there was no passageway between the two orchards. On the first day of apple-picking, Charlie drove the tractor (towing three trailers of wooden bins) along the seldom-used Findus Mine Road, a road that branched off from the Mitchell Highway. From packing shed to packing shed the distance was about three kilometres.

The relatively-new orchard contained a block of apple trees (containing several varieties of red apples) and a block of stone fruits (peaches, plums, and nectarines). Charlie soon learnt that the orchard was mainly a part-time venture for Paolo and his wife, Candela. Paolo's main source of income was derived from his employment in the security industry.

For the next seven and a half days, Charlie rarely used a ladder. Plus, the small trees were pruned with a notable degree of perfection. He regarded the physicality of this employment venture as a 'breeze' and comfortably filled eight bins of apples each day – and in less than eight hours. Paolo had also instructed each apple-picker that they could only fill a maximum of eight bins each day.

When the last of the apples were removed from the trees, Charlie was duly paid by Paolo in cash. No tax forms were filled in. Taking out a large wad of banknotes from his jeans pocket, Paolo soon placed $1200 (in $50 banknotes) in his hand. Charlie thought, not bad for seven and a half days work!

With nearly another week to fill in, Charlie managed to obtain several days of apple-picking at Comeforth Orchard, where he had previously worked. Eventually, the Granny Smith apple-picking season on Kevin and Alan's orchard commenced. The Granny Smith apples were picked in just two weeks. It was now the end of April.

At the time, most of the Granny Smith apples were sold primarily as eating apples. In future seasons, this particular variety would, once again, be generally sold as cooking apples. Orchardists would sell the majority of bins (of Granny Smith apples) to 'peelers' who would then mash the apples and use them for apple pies, baby food, apple puree, etc.

When they were sold mainly as eating apples, the harvesting of the Granny Smith apples wouldn't commence until at least mid-April. On some orchards, the harvesting wouldn't commence until the third week of April and the season could last through to the latter half of May.

When the Granny Smith apple was once more marketed as a cooking apple, customers (in fruit stores, supermarkets, etc.) would still purchase them as an *eating* apple, despite the distinctly tart-like taste. The Granny Smith apple season would now commence several weeks earlier: late March or early April. The picking season would now be completed by the end of April. Years later, new red apple varieties (Pink Ladies, Sundowners, Lady Williams, etc.) would emerge.

These varieties would be harvested (in the Orange area) anytime between the latter half of April and late May/early June).

The Granny Smith apples tended to taste sweeter when left on the trees longer; especially when picked mid to late May, as compared to the bitter tart-like taste when picked many weeks earlier. Unfortunately, a major problem with the later harvesting of Granny Smith apples was that they were more susceptible to bruising, particularly when the skins were wet, due to the morning dew/frost or rainfall. Fruit markets mostly wanted *unblemished* fruit.

As all the apples on Kevin and Alan's orchard had now been harvested, Charlie was now seeking more employment elsewhere within the Orange district. He soon discovered another nearby orchard seeking apple pickers.

Charlie drove along a narrow driveway with numerous potholes, until he came upon a poorly-constructed packing shed. He noticed that all the apple trees were quite large and poorly pruned. Charlie ventured cautiously into the packing shed, half-scared that it could collapse at any random time! He soon located the orchard owner: Alvin Trucker.

An over-talkative Alvin soon ensured an unnecessary long-winded conversation. Charlie soon sensed that there was something *odd* with his general demeanour. Annoyingly, as he conversed with him, Alvin would repeatedly nod his head and, even more annoying, constantly utter, "Yeah… yeah… yeah!"

For most of the conversation, Charlie felt that Alvin didn't comprehend what he was hearing – some sort of mental block, perhaps? As Charlie casually glanced in and around the hovel-like packing shed, he noticed a few other people who were mainly apple sorting. Charlie instantly recognised a few familiar faces – the infamous Woodstocks. He commenced apple picking the following day.

During these periods of extra employment, Charlie continued to reside in Kevin and Alan's orchard. Later that day, he was engaged in a light-hearted conversation with Rob (Kevin's son) and the *life and times* of Alvin Trucker soon dominated the discussion.

Rob readily agreed with Charlie that Alvin's orchard was in 'dire need of repair'. He further added that the orchard had largely been deemed by other local orchardists as the *Eighth Wonder of the World*. In stark contrast, Rob stated that Vernon (Alvin's brother) owned a well-organised and better-maintained orchard. He suggested to Charlie that it would be better for him to seek short periods of employment in Vernon's orchard instead of Alvin's. In the ensuing years, Charlie would indeed work on Vernon's orchard (picking only stone fruits) on several occasions.

In the evening, Charlie was in the tavern. He soon mentioned the name Alvin Trucker to fellow patrons. Jed and Spud had plenty to say about him! Jed immediately stated that he had worked on Alvin's orchard – once. In stark contrast, Spud had worked on Alvin's orchard on numerous occasions. He quickly declared to Charlie that Alvin was 'not the sharpest tool in the shed'. Other patrons nodded in unison.

In an attempt to emphasise his *not the sharpest tool in the shed* statement, Spud recalled the time that Alvin purchased expensive tins of powder. These tins of powder were emptied into a large spraying canister. The canister was then filled with water. Towed by a tractor, the mixture was supposed to *destroy* the unwelcomed blackberry bushes in the orchard.

Spud, who was sent out to spray the blackberry bushes, stated that the blackberries survived the chemical onslaught. He, on the other hand, was ill for a week. Later, Spud read the labels on the empty tins and realised that Alvin had spent several hundred dollars on the wrong type of chemicals!

The next morning, Charlie waited patiently (but not eagerly) for Alvin outside the dilapidated packing shed. Eventually, he could hear a little grey Fergie approaching – coughing, spluttering, and misfiring. As the tractor neared, Charlie noticed that Alvin had put his foot on the clutch, effectively running it in neutral. The tractor's wheels stopped rolling completely, less than a metre from Charlie's feet.

Charlie immediately grilled Alvin on the *braking capabilities* of this tractor. Casually and irritatingly dismissive, he suggested that one needs to 'plan ahead' before bringing the tractor to a complete halt. Charlie was not amused!

Just after Charlie had sat on the seat of the brakeless tractor, Alvin presented him with a tax form. A bemused Charlie quipped, 'What's this?'

On other orchards within the local district, he had never been given a tax form to fill out. Charlie was mildly agitated and deciding to be a little difficult, calmly stated to Alvin that he was illiterate. In response, Alvin just smiled and nodded his head!

After a brief silence, Charlie demanded:

'Alvin, you will need to provide me with assistance in completing this tax form. I'm illiterate!'

'Yeah, yeah, yeah … that's okay… most of my workers seem to have the same problem.'

With a pencil in hand, Alvin asked Charlie what his surname was. At the time, it was rare for itinerant workers to use their real surname on tax forms. Some members of the itinerant community even used different first names; Mustafa would become Michael, Chan would become Johnny, Gideon would become Jerry, etc.

Charlie's mind suddenly went blank. Glancing around for a burst of inspiration, the first thing that caught his eye was his Holden Kingswood sedan.

"Alvin … my last name is Holden!"

Next, Charlie was asked for his residential/mailing address. As itinerant fruit-pickers tended not to have a fixed address, a name of a caravan park or 'c/o of the post office' (in a particular town or city) would be provided.

"Care of Cobram (Victoria) Post Office" was the reply.

At the time, employees didn't need to provide a tax file number (TFN) on a tax form. A possibly misinformed Alvin, however, insisted that Charlie should state his TFN to him.

An exasperated Charlie blurted out, "Okay Alvin, my tax file number is 9… 8… 7… 6… 5… 4… 3… 2… 1!"

Finally, Alvin gave Charlie the tax form (and the pencil) and ordered that he needed to sign it.

'Alvin … where do I sign?'

Alvin pointed just to the right of 'Signature' and Charlie duly pencilled in a large 'X'.

'Alvin, sorry that my signature is a large X … but hey, I'm illiterate!'

With the paperwork completed, Charlie alighted from the tractor seat and stood on a metal grate of one of the bin trailers that separated the empty wooden bins. Alvin drove the tractor. As they passed through the dishevelled-looking orchard block, Charlie was horrified by what he saw, instantly recalling parts of the conversation with Rob (the previous day) who had stated that Alvin's orchard was in 'dire need of repair' and also widely regarded as the 'Eighth Wonder of the World'!

It was quite apparent to Charlie that the word 'organised' simply did not exist in Alvin's orchard. Apple-pickers seemed to be working wherever they wanted! Many apple trees still had plenty of fruit left on them – especially in the middle sections and on the tops of the trees.

Eventually, the tractor rolled to a halt. This section of the orchard had not been touched by other apple pickers. The trees were large and quite evidently, hadn't been pruned. As Charlie stood on the ground, he could see part of the packing shed – less than fifty metres away. For the past ten minutes, Alvin had practically been driving the tractor in an aimless direction!

Charlie was to offer his employment services on this orchard for only four days. He would deem the treacherous working conditions purely as a period of 'character building', opting to only fill four bins of apples (within seven hours) on each of these four days. It was early May.

Fortunately, Comeforth Orchard still had about three weeks of apple-picking employment left. By now, most itinerant fruit-pickers had departed from the area; they had decided to return to warmer climates – particularly in the state of Queensland. Still residing in Kelvin and Alan's orchard, Charlie drove to Comeforth Orchard each day, a journey of approximately ten minutes. As winter was just around the corner, the mornings were mostly cold and wet due to heavy dews or frost. During this time, Charlie would rarely commence apple-picking before 9.00 am.

Every morning, Charlie would park his vehicle in the parking area near the packing shed. After alighting from his vehicle, he would be greeted by the family pet, Jess (an adorable black and white border collie). Firstly, she would casually emerge from her kennel. Jess would then sprint across the concrete area in front of the packing shed and quite excitedly, greet Charlie. After several minutes of tummy rubbing and excessive tail wagging, she would return to the warmth of her homely kennel, located near the side door entrance of Ernie and Daphne's house. Meanwhile, the occupants of the household were fast asleep.

A major challenge for Charlie each morning was the momentous task of trying to get one of the grey Fergie tractors started. On most occasions, he would eventually succeed in getting one of the tractors to 'kick over'. Failure to start a tractor within ten minutes, however, required assistance and Charlie regarded Ernie as a *master* of starting an icy-cold tractor. This meant, however, that he would have to knock on the side door entrance of the house.

One bitterly cold morning, Charlie rapped loudly (several times) on the side door of the house. After several minutes, he finally heard some movement inside the house. The side door was suddenly opened. Before Charlie even had a chance to say anything, an airborne cat slammed hard against his chest! Fortunately, the cat landed fairly gently on the cemented surface on all four paws. The side door was then slammed shut.

Slightly stunned, Charlie paused for a few seconds. He knocked on the door again. Thirty seconds later the door was re-opened. A dishevelled-looking Ernie stood in the doorway wearing winter pyjamas. His hair was wildly tousled and his eyes were bloodshot – and barely opened. Shakily putting his spectacles on, he realised that Charlie was barely standing a metre away!

After a brief moment of silence, Ernie casually asked Charlie if he was near the door when he hurled the cat out. *Yes* was the definitive response. A partially-apologetic Ernie then proceeded to provide a feeble reason in explaining his actions – basically, too much cherry brandy the previous night.

Nevertheless, Ernie ventured out into the icy-cold and crisp air. A quarter of an hour later, he managed to get one of the tractors started and Charlie was soon on his way for another glorious day of apple picking.

In the ensuing years, Charlie would get to know Ernie, Daphne, and Jethro quite well. They were quite an intriguing family. He would also learn quite a good deal about them via other orchardists (within the Orange region) who widely regarded them as the wealthiest fruit growers within the district.

Over the years they had largely invested orchard profits into real estate. Several decades prior, they had purchased large tracts of land in and around the CBD of Orange. Eventually, these tracts of land would become prime real estate – especially the ones purchased by shopping centre developers. Similarly, they had purchased land in other NSW regional centres and several Sydney suburbs.

Despite their wealthy status, the family had largely chosen to adopt a relatively basic and simplistic lifestyle. Their home was an old three-bedroom weatherboard house that was built in the 1940s. The two vehicles in the carport (no garage was ever built) were at least 10 years old. Most farm machinery or equipment was *well-used*. The grey Fergie tractors were an obvious example.

Ernie, in particular, took the concept of a 'simplistic lifestyle' to a whole new level! His general dress sense consisted of well-used styles of clothing: partially ripped (or holey) off-white coloured singlets; faded and ripped tartan-styled shirts with missing buttons (occasionally replaced with safety pins); an old straw hat with many strips of straw missing (as he liked to chew on them); he regularly wore worn-out shoes; and, his favourite well-worn cardigan.

Ernie's main mode of transport within the orchard was an old Yamaha 70cc motorbike.

Requiring numerous basic repairs, he regarded it as his reliable 'put-put'. Most of the time, Ernie could only start the small motorbike by rolling it down a declining surface and then jump-starting it!

At some point during each day, Charlie would hear the easily recognisable sound of the 'put-put' approaching him. Ernie's daily social call. For the next half hour or so, he would casually chat with Charlie, picking apples and placing them directly into one of the wooden bins.

Daphne, on the other hand, would rarely leave the house. The only time that Charlie would see her was on Friday afternoons when he collected his weekly earnings, a process that would last for at least half an hour. In the guest room, Daphne (or Jethro) would provide Charlie and other apple pickers with either a hot beverage (coffee or tea) or non-alcoholic liquid refreshments, along with an assortment of cakes, biscuits, and other savoury delights. Charlie would generally be half-paid by a bank cheque; the other half of his weekly earnings were paid in cash.

As Comeforth Orchard was easily accessible from the Mitchell Highway, a large amount of fruit was sold from the packing shed. Passing motorists could easily see the large signs advertising, 'Fruit for Sale'. Ernie or Jethro would direct customers to park their vehicles on a grassy area, located near the side of the packing shed – never in front of the packing shed and there was a good reason for this.

Tractors, with four wooden bins (on two steel trailers) full of fruit, would stop at the cement-paved area in front of the packing shed. Before reaching this paved area, however, one would need to drive the fully laden tractor down a narrow and declining path. The decline was quite steep in sections. As well, the surface was largely rocky and uneven. If there was a vehicle parked in front of the packing shed, the tractor needed to be brought to a halt before proceeding down the rocky descent. Otherwise, once the fully laden tractor was proceeding down this path, it could only be brought to a halt – right in front of the packing shed. The tractor would have crashed into any parked vehicle within this space!

One afternoon, just as Charlie was approaching the packing shed, several people were wandering within the cemented area in front of the packing shed. Ernie and Jethro quickly moved them away from the path of the tractor. A minibus of excitable Japanese tourists had just entered the orchard several minutes earlier!

As Charlie brought the tractor to a halt, he was suddenly amidst an excitable aura of continual flashes and clicks. Charlie was quite amused by the instant 'celebrity status' that had been bestowed upon him. Even after he had turned the engine off and alighted from the tractor, the cameras were still clicking and flashing!

Jethro quietly made his way towards the centre of the packing shed. Meanwhile, still in front of the packing shed, Ernie was visibly exasperated by having to deal with a large group of excitable tourists! Charlie, though, soon came to the rescue and he started chatting with several of the tourists.

Charlie soon realised that the tourists had hoped there was a café. One of the young male tourists then enquired where the toilet was. A tactless Ernie retorted, 'Behind the packing shed … any tree will do!'

As the group wished to purchase large quantities of fruit, Jethro was soon assisting Ernie with the sales. Charlie sensed that Ernie was hoping that the group would soon be departing. But Daphne had other ideas.

After listening to the excitable commotion for more than ten minutes, Daphne suddenly emerged from the side door entrance of the house and greeted her foreign guests. Next, she invited them all into the house for afternoon tea. Rustic hospitality at its finest. Well done Daphne!

Ernie, meanwhile, was chewing on a strand of straw (taken from his hat) and tried to smile through gritted teeth. An amused Jethro quipped to Charlie as they went inside the house.

'Dad is chewing on that piece of straw quite vigorously … he'll do some damage to his teeth!'

Somewhat reluctantly, Ernie followed everyone back into the house.

Charlie had intended to go back into the orchard to pick two more bins of apples but decided to call it a day. Enjoying the social atmosphere in the spacious dining room, he chatted freely with several of the tourists who spoke a relatively good level of English. Most of the group, though, either spoke no English or only a limited amount.

An hour later, everyone was back outside again. For the next few minutes, Jess had a great time – lots of hugs, cuddles, and belly rubs from her newfound friends. In stark contrast, the cat was nowhere to be seen!

Eventually, the excitable and grateful tourists were aboard the minibus, along with many bags of fruit. They continued their journey eastwards along the Mitchell Highway towards the metropolis of Sydney. As the four of them bade the group of tourists farewell, Ernie sarcastically quipped, 'Well … that was a good sale!'

The apple-picking season on Comeforth Orchard came to an end during the last week of May. By now, the severe early-morning frosts had seen several mornings commence with minus Celsius degree temperatures. Charlie was now looking forward to the journey north to 'sunny' Queensland and warmer temperatures.

After departing from the region of Orange, one bitterly cold morning, Charlie arrived in the city of Brisbane (capital of Queensland) nearly twelve hours later. He had travelled a distance of 976 kilometres. After a one-week holiday in Brisbane, he then progressed onwards to the town of Gympie (170 kilometres north of Brisbane) to seek bean-picking employment.

9

Gimps and Gin

After leaving Brisbane, Charlie drove along the Bruce Highway for nearly two hours, until the outskirts of Gympie loomed into view. The town of Gympie, nestled within the Wide Bay-Burnett region of Queensland, is probably best known for its history of significant floods: the first one being recorded in 1870.

Periodic flooding mainly occurred due to excessive rainfall. This, in turn, resulted in the Mary River and its associated streams overflowing, particularly in the southern region of the town. The town was lesser known for its various vegetable harvests, especially its thriving hand-picked bean production (at the time).

Just after midday, Charlie drove into the Gympie Caravan Park, situated just off the highway and close to the town centre. A short time later, he erected his large canvas tent on a spacious area of thick mattress-like green vegetation. Although site fees (including powered sites) were quite cheap, the caravan park was barely half-full. As he hadn't eaten for several hours, Charlie was feeling quite peckish. Conveniently, a KFC restaurant was only about 400 metres

150

away. Fifteen minutes later, his hunger pangs were being effectively quelled.

In the evening, Charlie ventured to the communal area. It was quite clean and tidy. The spacious building block consisted of several pinball machines, a dartboard, a pool table, a community information board, and cooking facilities (a barbeque, a stove with four hot plates, two refrigerators, and food/drink cupboards).

As he used the cooking facilities, Charlie soon found himself engaged in light-hearted discussions with fellow travelling itinerants. Work-oriented themes, however, soon dominated the general conversation. He soon realised that there was widespread disillusionment with the employment situation within the local region – especially hand bean-picking.

Before using the cooking facilities, Charlie had noticed on the communal notice board an advertisement for bean pickers: 'Bean pickers wanted urgently. Telephone number xxxxxx. Ask for Gunther'. In a decidedly casual manner, he inquired whether anyone knew anything about this particular bean farm or if anyone had worked there previously. Charlie received an instant response – a largely negative one.

A young backpacking English couple informed Charlie that this particular bean farm had quite a *notorious* reputation. They had been working on Gunther's bean farm for nearly two weeks but left the job three days ago. On their last working day and along with several others, the pair angrily told Gunther *where he could stick his beans* – just before they walked off his bean farm.

Now in a state of excitable anger, the couple revealed that German-born Gunther was aged in his 60s and that he had an uncanny resemblance to 'Sergeant Schulz' (from the TV Series *Hogans Heroes*). They regarded Gunther's bean farm as being similar to a *stalag* – treating his employees more like prisoners. 'Commandant' Gunther was quite a tyrant!

Every morning, Gunther would arrive at the caravan park at 6.00 am – never early, never late – always punctual. During each day on his bean farm, Gunther would use an old wind-up alarm clock to signify and announce loudly when each rest/meal break started and finished. The young couple further claimed that he would yell hysterically at anyone who *disobeyed* his orders. In the evenings, Gunther drove his weary workers back to the caravan park in a minibus. He insisted that everyone had to be out of his vehicle within thirty seconds!

Upon further discussions with several other caravan park residents, it became quite clear to Charlie that bean-picking wasn't overly profitable. He learned that most of the hand-picked beans in the region were grown (in rows) on the slope of a hill. Towards the end of the evening, Sean, one of the tent dwellers, informed Charlie that he was going to seek employment at a bean farm (Kelville Farms) the next morning. This bean farm was located eight kilometres southwest of Gympie's CBD.

Sean revealed to Charlie that he had been residing in the coastal town of Byron Bay (northern New South Wales) for the past two years. Financially, he had been relying solely on unemployment benefits. Originally from the southern Sydney suburb of Cronulla, Sean further added that he had moved to northern New South Wales, mainly to fulfil his daily passion for surfing. As he shared a three-bedroom house with five other people, Sean boasted that relatively cheap living expenses allowed him to maintain an idyllic choice of lifestyle.

After two years, though, Sean decided he wanted to travel via a working itinerant lifestyle. Gympie was his first step in his quest to undertake a lengthy wanderlust journey.

The next morning, Sean drove out to Kelville Farms. A couple of hours later he returned, successful in obtaining a bean-picking position. Sean had also secured employment for Charlie as well. Although the commencement of employment was four days away, the pair could move into the living quarters (located in the packing shed) in two days.

On a Saturday morning, Sean and Charlie left the caravan park and a short time later they arrived at Kelville Farms. Charlie was soon introduced to Lionel, the owner of the bean farm. After a brief discussion, Sean and Charlie were shown the living quarters. Whilst the living quarters provided basic accommodation, it was obvious that it hadn't been used for quite a while. A lot of cleaning would be required. For the next couple of hours or so, the pair spent the time transforming their new abode into one that was much more homely.

Two days later, Lionel drove the two novices to a large block of beans. Working with four local bean pickers, each person was assigned a row of beans to pick. The beginning of the row was at the foot of the hill. Each individual was given several empty sacks. They were to be filled with selectively-picked beans as each individual made their way up the steep incline. Only beans over a certain length were supposed to be picked.

Both Sean and Charlie were provided with wet-weather gear: a pair of gumboots; canary-yellow coloured trousers; and, a canary-coloured coat (with a matching hood). Working in the rain was part of the job! Charlie and Sean slowly made their way up the hilly rows via several means: standing but with a bent back; on hands and knees (basically crawling); and, by sitting on their backsides – moving slowly up the steep incline.

By the late morning, the sky had turned a murky dark grey. A short time later, the heavens well and truly opened up. Although the ensuing rain was substantially torrential, the canary-coloured wet-weather gear did keep Charlie's other clothing relatively dry.

The empty sacks would be filled with beans several times a day. At the foot of the hill, there was a weigh-in station. Each sack was weighed and the weight (of the beans) was recorded manually. Each bean picker was responsible for carrying their full sacks of beans down the steep incline which could be quite muddy and slippery at times. Daily earnings were determined by the total weight, in kilograms, of beans picked.

By the end of the first day, Charlie realised that this money-making venture would barely be profitable. Due to his parlous financial situation at the time, he had no other choice but to persevere with this job; for at least a week. The local brigade, though, didn't fare that much better financially but they soon confessed to Charlie and Sean that their earnings from bean-picking were mainly a cash 'top-up' to their *disability* pensions.

The working conditions, for the next eight days, could be best described as 'character building'. Daily bouts of excessive amounts of rainfall ensured that the bean-picking venture was going to be quite hazardous at times. The terrain, especially between the rows, was virtually a long slippery dip. Maintaining a proper footing had become quite difficult in the soft and muddy conditions – even worse when one had to carry a full sack of beans to the weigh station, located near the foot of the hill. It was practically pointless trying to walk down the row with the sack of beans. It was much easier to just slide down the slippery slope with the sack of beans on your lap!

On one particular afternoon, the group of local bean-pickers deemed the treacherous inclement weather as being too severe to work in. In unity, they 'revolted' and decided to go home early. To complete the day's work, Lionel offered Sean and Charlie another form of employment: bean-sorting in the packing shed. The consistent and thunderous sound of the torrential rain on the corrugated tin roof, though, provided a less-than-ideal working environment – even drowning out the heavy noise of the bean-sorting machinery.

A substantial quantity of beans would continually move along the conveyor belt. Instead of moving smoothly along the belt, they tended to sporadically 'bounce' or 'leap' into the air at regular intervals. Charlie and Sean's task was to remove any beans that were either rotten or had major blemishes on them. Initially, Charlie's eyes would follow the bouncing beans as they moved along the conveyor belt. Occasionally, he would lose his sense of balance as he succumbed to the effects of mild vertigo.

Sean then suggested to Charlie to just look straight over the bouncing beans occasionally, straightening his balance, instead of tilting his body too far to the right. This idea was partially successful, but Charlie noticed that Sean would also occasionally lose his balance. Fortunately, this unpleasant task only lasted for two hours – the first and *last* time that Charlie sorted beans.

After eight days of bean-picking, Charlie decided it was time to move to greener pastures. One of the local bean pickers on this bean farm had informed him that the tomato-picking season had just commenced near the small town of Gin Gin: 181 kilometres north of Gympie. With $300 saved, Charlie was soon driving on the Bruce Highway again.

Two hours later, Charlie arrived in Gin Gin and headed straight for the town's only hotel. After consuming a meal, he soon struck a conversation with several itinerant workers. Charlie soon learnt that they were all working on a tomato farm, located six kilometres east of Gin Gin. All of them were also residing in the local caravan park (now known as the Puma Gin Gin Caravan Park and Roadhouse).

After departing from the hotel, Charlie drove to the caravan park. After paying a weekly powered-site fee, he pitched his tent. The caravan park contained a small community area which included cooking facilities, a refrigerator, and a large table with long bench seats. In the evening, whilst preparing dinner, Charlie conversed with many of the campers who were employed on several different fruit/vegetable farms.

One of the itinerant campers, Boris, was working on a small family-owned farm that harvested a variety of different vegetables (peas, beans, baby pumpkins, squashes, etc). Every evening, he would bring a milk crate of vegetables to the communal area, to be shared amongst the itinerant workers. Tim and Stuart, who Charlie had met earlier in the hotel, assured him that he would secure an immediate start at their place of employment: Martino's Tomato Farm.

Early the next morning, before 6.00 am, Charlie drove the pair to the tomato farm. Upon alighting from the vehicle, Tim introduced Charlie to the tomato farm's owner: Ronnie Martino. Ronnie quickly assured him that he had an immediate start and several minutes later gave Charlie *two* tax forms to fill in.

Ronnie casually stated to Charlie that he didn't care what he wrote on each form! He did suggest to him, however, to write on the second form that he was married with five children – a ploy to pay less tax as possible.

At the time, seasonal work was taxed at the normal standard tax rates. This meant that there was a tax threshold, where no tax was paid. Dependents (e.g. wife, offspring, etc.) could be used as a tax deduction. Two years later, the federal government introduced a flat tax rate of thirteen percent on the total weekly income earned, for all itinerant seasonal employment (such as fruit or vegetable picking).

Each morning, for the next ten days, Charlie (and other willing participants) would be in the tomato paddock before 6.00 am. Sunrise hadn't yet begun. Tomato picking wouldn't commence until there was sufficient light, mainly to distinguish the difference between a green tomato and a red one! The tomato picking was paid by piece rate: $1.00 per full bucket of tomatoes. Alas, each workday was of short duration, finishing between 11.00 am and midday.

After the arduous morning toil, the majority of the itinerant tomato pickers headed for one particular location: the hotel. Everyone (including Charlie) was either on *unemployment benefits* or an *invalid pension.*

Earnings from tomato picking were spent on alcohol consumption, hotel meals, and 'punting' (gambling on racehorses/greyhounds). The hotel had a betting agency (known as a TAB).

Upon entering the hotel, Charlie would firstly purchase a beer. After consuming it within a few minutes, he would order lunch and purchase another beer. Throughout the afternoon and evenings, the hotel pool table would be in constant use. Charlie, however, would rarely play a game of pool. Instead, he preferred to spend the afternoon punting on horse races and consuming more glasses of beer. Charlie's keen interest in punting led him to regularly converse with an elderly gentleman, Tom. Despite being aged in his early-

70s, he still enjoyed the lure of the nomadic itinerant lifestyle.

Although Tom owned a house in the city of Brisbane, he was not contented with the leisurely lifestyle of a retiree. For 6-8 months of the year, Tom preferred a mixture of travel (both in Australia and abroad) and 'paid outdoor exercise' (fruit/vegetable picking). Besides being a keen punter, he had previously owned or part-owned racehorses. In his younger days, Tom had been a jockey for over twenty years.

Nearly every afternoon in the TAB room of the hotel, Tom would place quite a few bets, solely on thoroughbred racing – and, with a relatively high success rate. As Charlie (at the time) had aspirations of becoming a professional punter, he would regularly discuss with Tom the process of analysing the data from thoroughbred racing form guides. The primary aim was to transform the output into 'meaningful' punting knowledge.

Charlie learned that Tom had developed and applied his own betting system over several years, based on several key factors: whether to back a horse for a win only or a place bet; deciding which races to bet on or which ones to ignore; and, selecting the best type of betting for a particular race (win/place, quinellas, trifectas, all-up bets, etc.).

Over the next few months, Charlie would devise his own punting system. He would largely base it on particular statistical information (success/strike rate on certain tracks, race distance, race conditions, etc.) of each racehorse in a particular race meeting. Charlie would further develop his punting system by analysing race patterns and trends. Occasionally, he would gain *inside* information from 'reliable' sources. In the ensuing years, Charlie would regularly make a tidy profit, especially when placing bets at thoroughbred racetracks.

Although Charlie was enjoying his time in Gin Gin, the lure of a tropical paradise (i.e. above the Tropic of Capricorn) was constantly on his mind. After ten days, the tomato-picking employment situation reached a critical point. The next patches of tomatoes were not ready to be picked for at least five days. Yet again, Charlie was driving along the Bruce Highway, towards the tropical paradise of Bowen in North Queensland.

10

Return to Paradise

After departing from Gin Gin in the late afternoon, Charlie had planned to drive through the tranquil and calmness of the night right through to the tropical town of Bowen: a distance of 791 kilometres. An hour and a half into the journey, however, as he was driving through the small quaint town of Bororen, a large wooden structure soon caught his eye. The Bororen Hotel. Except for the roofing, everything else was constructed of wood. Unique in style and finely polished.

Developing a sudden thirst, Charlie parked his vehicle outside the hotel and ventured inside. To complement the outer appearance, the interior decor was also largely influenced by high-quality timber with elaborately designed floorboards and walls. The ceiling was also constructed of wood. His original intention was to just have one or two refreshing alcoholic beverages but the hotel patrons were quite chatty!

As dusk crept in, a comfortably-seated and relaxed Charlie changed his mind. Instead, he decided to stay in the nearby caravan park that night where the price of an 'overnight van' (caravan) was quite cheap. Over the ensuing years, Charlie would have several overnight stopovers in this particular caravan park as he travelled to and from Bowen. After parking his vehicle inside the caravan park, he returned to the Bororen Hotel.

Over the next several hours and with the 'amber fluid' (beer) freely flowing, Charlie spent most of the night engaged in earnest conversation with several local patrons and other overnight travellers who were mostly staying at the motel next door to the hotel.

At one point during the general conversation, Charlie revealed that his original intention was to drive right through the night and onto Bowen. The local patrons, in particular, were horrified by this revelation! They quickly explained to Charlie, several potential hazards of driving along the Bruce Highway during the night:

1. He would be sharing the highway with a large number of speeding trucks, many of them travelling more than 120 km/h.
2. There was a high risk of unwelcomed clashes with wallabies or kangaroos, hopping around aimlessly, or stopping suddenly on the road (particularly when blinded and/or disoriented by a vehicle's bright lights).
3. The risk of the vehicle breaking down and not being able to contact anyone for assistance.
4. Plagues of insects practically glue themselves to the vehicle's windscreen or are embedded in unprotected radiator fins (Charlie's vehicle had a relatively large radiator grill which had spaces large enough to allow

numerous insects to easily make it right through to the feeble fins).

The next morning, just after 6.00 am, Charlie awoke from a restful slumber. Half an hour later, he was driving on the Bruce Highway once again. Whilst plagues of insects were nowhere to be seen and no marsupials hopping aimlessly across the highway, Charlie did come across numerous blood-spattered carcasses on both the road and the shoulders (of the road).

On several occasions, Charlie had to slow down, basically zigzagging across the road to avoid any contact with the carnage on the road. Throughout the night, oversized vehicles (semi-trailers and road trains) with large steel bull bars (also known as push bumpers or 'roo' bars) hurtled up and down the highway, mercilessly barrelling down any unfortunate creatures within their path!

After an eight-hour journey, Charlie arrived at the southern outskirts of Bowen. Four kilometres, south of Bowen, he entered the Edgecombe Village Caravan Park (now the Bowen Village Caravan Park). Charlie had previously stayed in this caravan. Upon entering the office complex, he was greeted by the new owners: Norm and Mona.

Informing the new owners that he had previously stayed in this caravan park, Charlie inquired what had happened to the previous owner: 'Garden Gnome' Graham. Mona informed him that Graham (and his wife), two months ago, decided to become *grey nomads*. The 'grey nomads' are retirees who have chosen to travel throughout rural Australia. In the vast countryside, they could be seen towing a caravan or they travelled in motor homes (such as minivans or large buses) – often at a leisurely pace.

For economic reasons, Charlie decided to join the tenting community as unpowered sites (at the time) cost a paltry $35 per week. Hiring a caravan started at $90 per week. As he had not pre-arranged any employment before he arrived in Bowen, Charlie's financial situation required 'tight fiscal restraint'. Nevertheless, he was quite confident that he would secure tomato-picking employment within a week.

That evening, Charlie made his presence known in the communal area. The communal area was mostly occupied by fellow tent-dwellers and he soon learnt that they were all currently employed. 'Kiwi' Pete, Dan, and Mal were all employed on a tomato farm (owned by Leith Prince) which was located just a few kilometres from the caravan park. New Zealander Pete assured Charlie that he would be able to secure employment on this tomato farm within the next two or three days.

The next morning, Charlie went to the Department of Social Security (DSS) to deliver his completed *Unemployment* form and thus, receive his fortnightly payment. This would be the last payment he would receive, before commencing employment in the Bowen region.

[Note: the DSS would later merge with CES (Commonwealth Employment Services) and be renamed Centrelink].

This was the standard practice amongst the itinerant fruit-picking community. The vast majority of itinerant workers would already be on unemployment benefits before they arrived in the Bowen region. As most of them would also commence employment within a week, this would be the last *Unemployment* form that they would hand into the DSS – for a few months, at least.

After departing from the local DSS office, Charlie drove directly to Leith Prince's tomato farm. At the packing shed, he was introduced to Brett 'Sweat' Prince (Leith's brother). Charlie later learned that Brett had acquired the nickname 'Sweat' due to his reluctance to actively participate in anything that required arduous physical toil! Brett informed him that he could commence tomato-picking the next morning. Although Leith owned the tomato farm outright, Charlie would never meet him.

In the evening, Charlie informed the trio (Pete, Dan, and Mal) that he would be commencing employment at Leith Prince's tomato farm the next morning. Dan informed Charlie that employment was quite plentiful: usually six days a week. He further added that from a financial point of view, the tomato-picking venture would generally be quite prosperous.

Mal, however, informed Charlie that there was a major 'obstacle' to overcome: Milton (the paddock boss). In unison, the trio largely regarded Milton as an idiot. They wouldn't elaborate to Charlie the reasons why but calmly informed him, 'You'll soon find out why!'

The next morning, all four of them travelled together in Mal's vehicle to the tomato farm. The highlight of the ten-minute journey was the crossing through the dry river bed of Menilden Creek. For at least a few months of the year, vehicles were able to drive on one of several tracks across the breadth of the waterway (or one of its connecting tributaries). During the cyclone/monsoonal season, this waterway was regularly filled with a large volume of water and was also fast-flowing.

After alighting from the vehicle, Charlie was soon introduced to Milton. Aged in his late forties, he was of a stocky build but relatively short in stature (1.70 metres or 5'7"). As Milton was wearing a sleeveless denim shirt, tattoos of small butterflies were visible on his upper arms. The tattoos reminded a semi-amused Charlie of his early teenage years when he used to buy packets of bubble gum that included a temporary tattoo – easily washed off with water.

Just after they shook hands, a tactless Milton proceeded to inform Charlie of *certain expectations* on this tomato farm: a minimum number of full buckets had to be picked each day; one needed to be 'gentle' with the tomato bushes; and, to only pick the 'right' tomatoes (a.k.a select picking). Quite cynically, Charlie just kept nodding his head, occasionally responding with the words, 'Yeah, no worries!'

Before the commencement of any tomato-picking, the entire group had to gather around Milton. With the aid of two buckets, both filled with several tomatoes, he began his daily 'pep' talk.

'The first bucket contains the *good* tomatoes; you fill your buckets with these. The second bucket contains the *bad* tomatoes; they don't go into your buckets … too many of these … you're sacked!'

After two hours of treacherous toil, the entire crew stopped for the thirty-minute morning tea break. Memories of the previous tomato-picking season were already haunting Charlie – especially the chronic back pain and the severe stiffening of the legs (particularly when one was resting). Milton, however, had spent most of the first two-hour work period in a 4WD vehicle – power-napping.

During the first part of the rest break, a rested Milton mostly chatted with Mal about music. They were both accomplished guitarists. Milton, in particular, had played guitar in several bands over the past three decades. These bands had also toured extensively throughout Australia and New Zealand, performing in numerous cities and towns.

In the latter half of the first rest break, Milton was mainly conversing with Charlie. Holding a half-filled plastic bottle, which contained what looked like custard-flavoured milk, he began to prattle on about his personal 'body-building' regime!

The flavoured 'milk' was, supposedly, a high-protein liquid for *muscle enhancement*. A bored Charlie listened patiently (but was now eager to return to work) to the key aspects of Milton's body-building regime which centred on calorie-controlled diets and power-lifting/weights training. Although Milton had solidly built 'fat' arms, he wasn't overly muscular – and his prominent beer belly still required a fair bit of work. As Milton continued to ramble on, poor Charlie was looking for an escape route. His fellow itinerants were certainly no help. They had all moved well away from the pair!

Eventually, the first rest break came to an end and everyone returned to the tomato field. Except for Milton. He returned to his vehicle for another power nap – having not recovered from his daily 5.30 am gym workout.

Occasionally, Milton would conduct bucket checks, ensuring that the *peasants* were doing the 'right thing'. Whilst resting in his vehicle, he would get word from the packing shed (via an audibly loud CB radio) informing him that an excess of defective, over-ripened, or rotten tomatoes was on the sorting conveyor belts.

Milton would then gingerly alight from the vehicle, cursing loudly as he walked to the block of tomatoes. 'Fucking useless peasants' was one of his favourite phrases! Milton hated doing bucket checks and he would constantly moan about the *severe* strain on his back. One wonders what Milton was 'power-lifting' at his gym!

Each day, Milton would routinely threaten all tomato-pickers with the possibility of job dismissal. The itinerants, however, knew they could easily obtain employment elsewhere. One afternoon, whilst Milton was resting and *snoring* in his work vehicle, several of the itinerant workers (including Charlie) came upon an old patch of rockmelon/cantaloupe vines amongst the tomato bushes - still bearing fruit. An opportunity to quickly fill a substantial number of buckets had arisen. The bottom half of the bucket was filled with rockmelons and the top half was filled with tomatoes!

About an hour later, the rockmelons landed on the conveyor belts! Moments later, the tomato-pickers could hear an irate Milton. As he listened to what was being conveyed to him, Milton swore repeatedly and *loudly*. Visibly angry, he slammed the door of the vehicle. With shoulders up and chest puffed out, he stormed towards the itinerant collective and checked numerous full buckets – no rockmelons were to be found.

In desperation, Milton decided to employ bullying tactics, accusing certain individuals directly. Although everyone was aware of the mischievous escapade, a united tomato-picking crew 'played dumb' and denied any knowledge of the recent occurrence. After quite a long-winded bout of huffing and puffing, Milton decided to retreat to his vehicle – resuming his afternoon nap.

Charlie had originally intended to stay on this particular tomato farm until the end of the tomato-picking season. Milton's regular deplorable behavior, however, gradually took its toll. With a few weeks remaining, Charlie (along with many of the other tomato-pickers) decided to seek greener 'pastures'.

Outside the work environment, Charlie enjoyed the camaraderie within the caravan park. In the late afternoon and continuing into the evening, the majority of the tent-dwelling community would congregate in the centrally-located communal area to share their daily 'adventures' in the fields (and in the packing sheds).

Although the majority of the group was picking tomatoes, others worked on farms that produced other fruits such as capsicums/peppers, rockmelons, watermelons, chillies, baby bananas, and squashes. In the communal area on most evenings, milk crates were filled with a variety of local produce, mainly for the tent-dwelling community to use.

The 9.00 pm curfew within the communal area, as in the previous year, was still enforced. This included the television being switched off at this time. On many occasions, however, the television had either been switched off earlier or the volume had been decreased significantly. The vast majority of the tent-dwelling community preferred to be engaged in earnest conversations, often of a boisterous nature but one that was still in a light-hearted manner.

Nevertheless, the 'big fella' (Norm) would arrive at the communal area (riding a bright blue quad bike) just after 9.00 pm, enforcing the curfew if necessary. During the day, he would regularly ride his quad bike within the caravan park grounds. Norm seldom walked. His wife, Mona, also rarely walked. She made her way around, within the confines of the caravan park – on a bright-red quad bike.

During this particular tomato-picking season, Norm had a mild heart attack. In response, his GP (doctor) told him that he should "relax" and to "take it easy" – advice that probably led to Norm having a mild heart attack in the first place. Anyway, Norm did indeed *take it easy* for the next few weeks, rarely leaving the lounge room couch in the office/residence building complex. Norm wouldn't even ride his quad bike – too much physical stress on the body.

Throughout the tomato-picking season, Charlie would drink copious amounts of alcohol (especially beer) every day; a trend that he would prevail with for well over a decade. Just after consuming a sumptuous fried breakfast meal (sausages, bacon, mushrooms, sliced potatoes, eggs, tomatoes, and toast), Charlie would be downing his first beer for the day (largely as an aid to digest the 'morning feast')!

In stark contrast, the rest of the tent-dwelling community generally skipped breakfast or ate very little. Just before 6.00 am each morning, though, Charlie (still in his tent) would hear water-gargling noises from nearby tenting residents – the sounds of homemade bongs being used.

Additionally, the sound of a ring-pull (from a can of warm beer) could be heard being opened inside Dan's tent!

Around 6.30 am, as Charlie cooked his mammoth breakfast in the communal area, the dynamic trio of Pete, Mal, and Dan would each be having a cigarette or a marijuana joint, along with a large mug of coffee. Like Charlie, each of them would also consume a beer, just before travelling to the tomato farm. Kiwi Pete attempted to justify his breakfast routine to others in the communal area by referring to beer as a *heart starter* and marijuana use as an *attitude adjuster*. He further added that these morning vices were a necessity when one is faced with the daily adversity of life in the tomato field – a coping mechanism in dealing with the irksome antics of Milton.

Each morning, the four of them would arrive at the tomato paddock in a partially-dazed stupor or a mild state of 'social inebriation'. They weren't alone! Most of the tomato-picking crew would be in a similar state. In turn, Milton would be quite upset with the group's lack of attentiveness to his daily 'pep' talk. The strong intertwining odour of alcohol and marijuana that dominated the morning air further irked him! Nevertheless, a few minutes later, the 'peasants' would casually amble towards the tomato bays to commence a day's tomato-picking. Milton returned to the vehicle – for his first power nap.

During Charlie's four-month stay in the caravan park, he and several other members of the tenting community would learn a valuable lesson – tents, candles, and alcohol do not mix well together. One evening, just as dusk was settling in, Charlie was reading a book inside his tent via candlelight. He had already consumed quite a few cans of beer.

Feeling sleepy, Charlie closed the book and decided to lie down, intending to just have a short nap. Several minutes later, he was groggily awoken by frantic yelling and shouting behind the back of his tent. He could feel the flames – just behind his head. Seconds later, Charlie was drenched with a large amount of water, and the fire was quickly extinguished.

Fortunately, Charlie wasn't harmed but there was now a large gaping hole in the back of his canvas tent! This would be the first and *last* time he would ever have a candle in a tent. From that moment on, Charlie would only ever use a battery-operated torch/flashlight inside a tent. Initially, a large black sheet of plastic covered the back of his tent. A few days later, the sheet was replaced with a large piece of near-matching canvas which was machine-stitched by a friend of Mona's.

Over the next two months, Charlie's close encounter would be the first of several tent fires. Ken, a New Zealand national, was the next individual to have a candle mishap. The front section of his tent caught on fire, destroying the fly screen and part of the front tent flaps. He swiftly extinguished the fire on his own and, fortunately, he too was not harmed. Then it was Dan's turn.

One evening, Dan accidentally knocked over a candle, setting the floor of his tent on fire. Although he managed to quickly extinguish the flames with items of clothing, there was still a large hole in the floor of his tent. Numerous clothing items had been badly singed. But worse was to follow – yet another tent fire.

Kiwi Pete had fallen asleep inside his tent with a candle still alight – next to an aerosol can of insect repellent. Sometime later, the heated can *exploded*. The loud noise caught the attention of several other tent-dwelling residents and they soon extinguished the fire. However, unlike the others (Charlie, Ken, and Dan), Pete was less fortunate. He would suffer burns on one side of his face and extensive burns to both of his hands (and partially to his forearms).

Over several months, the loss of skin and subsequent scarring on Pete's face slowly healed.

At the time, both of his hands were bandaged and he was unable to work for the next three weeks. When Pete did finally return to the tomato field he wore cotton gloves, improvised to fit over the now-thinner bandages. After six more weeks, Pete was able to work without the bandages – but scarring on his hands could still be seen.

Meanwhile, about halfway through Charlie's four-month stay in the caravan park, he informed Norm and Mona that he wished to upgrade to caravan accommodation when one became available. The recent tent fires had partially prompted him to consider alternative means of accommodation. There was another reason, however, magpie 'swooping' season had just begun.

In reality, it was just the *one* magpie that created the havoc – especially for the tent-dwelling community. This particular magpie soon earned the nickname *Mad Maggie.* She would frequently swoop down, snapping her jaws just millimetres or centimetres from an individual's head! One of her favourite perching places was a medium-sized palm tree – near Charlie's tent.

As a cautious Charlie slowly emerged from his tent, he would first look upwards, towards the top of the palm tree to see if Mad Maggie was perched there. If she was, Charlie would throw small stones at her in an attempt to encourage her to relocate elsewhere. The ruse, however, backfired badly and Mad Maggie soon developed an intense dislike for Charlie! Just after emerging from his tent, she would glide (quite aggressively) towards his head and often from behind him. Charlie, though, soon learned to duck – quickly.

In stark contrast and after a sustained period of caution and trust, Kiwi Pete became *friends* with Mad Maggie. He would regularly feed her young brood. Hesitant at first, the young magpies would cautiously accept gifts of food placed near his tent. Eventually, they would eat birdseed out of Pete's bandaged hand! Mad Maggie, meanwhile, was not so trusting. She would only accept food that was placed a reasonable distance from his tent. Upon hearing complaints from other caravan park residents (especially the tent dwellers) of regular swooping attacks from Mad Maggie, Pete gleefully bragged, 'She's never swooped down on me!'

One Saturday afternoon, tent-dwelling Jim (a Canadian national), became trapped in a public telephone booth, located just outside the caravan park. A persistent Mad Maggie kept swooping on him every time he tried to leave the phone booth. In desperation, Jim rang the caravan park office to inform Norm that he was trapped in the telephone booth! Before this moment, there had been numerous complaints to Norm and Mona. Mad Maggie's constant and aggressive swooping manoeuvres had recently extended throughout the caravan park. Complaints were largely met with the promise: 'We'll take care of the situation!'

A short time later, Ben (one of Norm and Mona's sons) approached the telephone booth with a loaded rifle. He fired a shot at Mad Maggie and she flew away from the vicinity. Ben was adamant that the bullet had hit her. Jim was not so sure. Mad Maggie would not be seen for the next two days.

On the third day, though, a familiar sight emerged above the camping area. It soon became clear that one of her 'dipped' wings had been damaged. Despite the damaged wing, Mad Maggie soon resumed her aggressive swooping escapades – mainly in the camping area. She might have been looking for Jim! Several days later, someone from a 'Wildlife Rescue and Care' group came to the caravan park. Setting several traps, he aimed to capture her humanely.

Naturally, there was a fair bit of scepticism within the tent-dwelling community as to whether the traps would work successfully or not. But two days later, Mad Maggie was finally captured. Relieved caravan park residents were once more able to roam around freely, having not to constantly look up for the 'black silhouette' flying menacingly above them. Meanwhile, Mad Maggie's young brood continued to be fed by their *de facto mum*, still eating birdseed and other titbits out of Pete's bandaged hand!

Several days later, Charlie relocated to a fully-contained caravan. His weekly rent was now $90 per week, a substantial increase from paying $35 per week. The caravan had an air-conditioner where the usage cost was included in the weekly rent. For the next few weeks, he would use it regularly. Now feeling more relaxed, Charlie mostly kept to himself and rarely communicated with neighbouring caravan-dwellers. He still kept in contact with the tent-dwelling community, visiting the communal area several times a week.

With a few weeks of the tomato-picking season remaining, Charlie sought new employment opportunities. Most of the tomato-picking crew, who had started the season on Leith Prince's tomato farm, were now employed on other tomato farms. Milton remained – unfortunately. Two days later, Charlie commenced employment on a tomato farm located four kilometres north of Bowen's town centre.

11

Troppo Season in Tropicana

Although caravan life was more comfortable for Charlie, social interaction with neighbouring caravan dwellers would be quite limited. One of his next-door neighbours was a young Murri (an indigenous Australian) woman: June. Employed in one of the local tomato packing sheds, she was a quiet lady and rarely spoke to any of the other caravan park residents. Whenever Charlie said hello and asked how she was, June would only acknowledge him with a shy smile and one-word replies: 'hello' and 'good'.

On most days, June would work for at least ten hours. On several occasions, she had fallen asleep in the late evenings, leaving the television set on. Against the quiet serenity of the night air, it would be audible enough for nearby caravan-dwellers to hear. The noise of her television set never bothered Charlie. A combination of a hard day's toil and a substantial intake of alcohol ensured that he slept well each night! Unfortunately, several complaints from a caravan-dwelling couple (residing opposite June's caravan) were made to the caravan park owners.

Bill and Julia, a retired couple from metropolitan Melbourne, would complain to Norm and Mona (the caravan park owners) regarding the 'issue' of the television noise, instead of just confronting June directly (and gently). Charlie soon learnt that Mona, in particular, had already taken a dislike to the retired couple. She had already branded them *compulsive whingers* as they had previously made numerous complaints: conditions of the amenities block; the numerous squashed cane toads on the roadways; falling coconuts (from nearby palm trees); and, the *behaviour* of other caravan park residents!

Although Mona and Norm largely ignored their complaints, the couple would not be easily deterred. One late afternoon, the pair decided to take matters further – they organised a petition. Firstly, they knocked on Charlie's caravan door. Through the locked screen door, he could see that Julia was holding a clipboard (with an attached sheet of paper) and a pen. Charlie sensed that they wanted to come inside his caravan. That wasn't going to happen!

Before Charlie could utter a word, an exasperated Bill began to prattle about the ongoing issue of the audible level of June's television in the late evenings. Although Charlie could hear the television set, the noise level was quite low. A perplexed Charlie instantly retorted, 'What noise… what are you talking about?'

Charlie calmly stated to them that the noise of June's television had never disturbed his sleep. The irksome (and persistent) couple, nevertheless, insisted that he *must* have heard it, even attempting to verbalise him at times. Standing his ground, Charlie soon ordered the pair to leave. Quite reluctantly, Bill and Julia did eventually leave – but only to knock on the door of another neighbouring caravan.

Although Charlie seldom spoke to other nearby caravan-dwellers, he would still learn of interesting tidbits of gossip. His other next-door neighbour was a single mother with six children, all residing in the one large caravan. A popular and vicious rumour, circulating within the caravan park, suggested that each of her six children had a different father! According to gossip-mongers, the woman (aged in her mid-thirties) was a long-term welfare recipient. She rarely spoke to any of the other caravan park residents.

On the other side of the roadway, opposite Charlie's caravan and next door to Bill and Julia resided a single male: Rupert. Aged in his early-50s, he was a quiet-natured fellow but a near-constant smiling one.

Similar to June, Rupert was also employed at one of the local tomato packing sheds. Although he regularly conversed with Bill and Julia, any conversation with Charlie was generally limited.

'Hello, how are you?'

'Good.'

'It's a nice day.'

'Yes, it is.'

'How's work going?'

'Good!'

Surprisingly, one particular Saturday afternoon, the conversation between the pair expanded beyond the simple pleasantries. As if some sort of barrier had been broken, he invited Charlie into his residential abode for a cup of coffee. Rupert was a teetotaller; he didn't keep any alcohol in his caravan. As Charlie made his way through the caravan entrance, he was instantly met with numerous photos, newspaper clippings, and posters on all walls – and even the refrigerator door – of a star female tennis player at that time (Martina Hingis).

A shocked Charlie tried his best to hide his sense of bemusement with what he instantly deemed as an *unhealthy obsession* with the 'Swiss Miss'. Whilst Rupert was eager to impart his intimate knowledge of the tennis star, Charlie was keen to change the subject to anything not tennis-related. After listening to Rupert's enthusiastic babble for more than ten minutes, he was now devising an escape plan. Upon finishing his coffee, Charlie politely declared to Rupert, 'I better go… I have things to do.' He never went inside Rupert's caravan again!

Further down from Bill and Julia's caravan was a couple aged in their mid-thirties: Darren and Trudy. The itinerant fruit-picking (and recently-married couple) were regularly intoxicated in the evenings. As a result, they could be quite volatile towards each other at times. Strangely though, at some point, the quarrelling would just suddenly come to an abrupt end. After a sustained period of relative silence, loud audible groans of ecstasy, accompanied by plenty of huffing and puffing, could be easily heard by nearby neighbours!

As the weeks went by, Darren and Trudy's constant quarrelling escalated to a level of increased volatility. Cutlery, pots, and pans were now being regularly hurtled against the walls of the caravan – mainly by Trudy. The *neighbourhood-watch* duo (Bill and Julia) had already complained to Mona on several occasions. Eventually, Norm (with assistance from his two sons) decided to evict the volatile couple.

Several years later, Charlie would cross paths with Darren and Trudy, who were still residing in the Bowen region. He was surprised that they were still together – albeit, with two small children. Compared to the last time that he had seen them, however, their behaviour seemed to be much calmer and physically, they were far healthier-looking.

Residing next-door to Darren and Trudy was another couple: Joe and Mary. Aged in their mid-forties, Joe and Mary were semi-retired and were 'following the sun'. They had only recently decided to adopt an itinerant lifestyle.

Every Saturday afternoon another couple, Harry and Sally (who resided within the township of Bowen), would drive to the caravan park to visit them. Initially, it appeared to the casual outside observer that all four of them got on quite well with each other.

After a substantial intake of alcohol, though, Harry and Mary tended to fall asleep in the caravan annexe (an enclosed awning). Subsequently, Joe and Sally then moved into the caravan. Upon closing the door, they would quietly converse with each other for quite a while – and, that's how the affair started.

One night, Joe and Mary were engaged in a heated argument. Besides the audible foul language, plenty of pots and pans were being hurled around within the caravan. An hour later, a taxi arrived. Mary was leaving Joe.

Joe remained in Edgecombe Village Caravan Park. Mary had moved to another caravan park.

Several nights a week, Sally would be in Joe's caravan. On these nights, he would first drive to a rendezvous point and return to the caravan park with her. This escapade was to continue for several weeks. During this time, Charlie hadn't seen or heard anything from Harry. Then, late one night!

Charlie was fast asleep when, suddenly, he was awoken by what sounded like a loud explosion. Moments later, Charlie heard the roar of a four-wheel-drive being reversed at high speed. In a sleep-deprived state, he went outside to investigate the commotion. Other caravan park residents had already gathered around Joe's vehicle.

One side of Joe's vehicle had been smashed in significantly; the side windows were either cracked or in pieces. An angry Joe was soon on his mobile phone, talking to a local police officer. A terrified Mary remained inside the caravan. The next day, Harry was arrested and charged over the incident. After his court appearance, he subsequently moved out of the local area, driving southwards along the Bruce Highway.

Charlie, meanwhile, had commenced employment at another tomato farm, located about four kilometres north of the town centre. He would be employed at this particular tomato farm for the next five tomato-picking seasons.

On his first day of employment, Charlie would not meet the tomato-farm owner until the early afternoon. As he was filling a bucket of tomatoes, Charlie was approached by a tall lanky fellow wearing dark-blue denim shorts, a matching dark-blue *King Gee* shirt, and a large dark-grey Akubra (a hat made of rabbit fur pelt with a wide brim). He firmly shook Charlie's hand and authoritatively announced, 'John's the name – John Wayne.'

For the remaining duration of the tomato-picking season, John would regularly visit the tomato field, several times a day. He would occasionally fill a few buckets with tomatoes for each tomato-picker. In the mid-afternoon, on most days,

John would be seen driving through a particular tomato field, mainly checking irrigation systems or assessing the ripeness of a patch (or block) of tomatoes. On the seat of his four-wheel-drive vehicle was a small esky – containing a six-pack of beer. He would *regularly* be seen with one hand on the steering wheel and a cold beer in the other!

Charlie's fellow itinerant tomato-pickers were quite a *diverse* group. The crew consisted of twenty-two people. Whilst seven of them (including Charlie) were Australian-born, the rest of the crew were either born in New Zealand, the United Kingdom, Ireland, Tonga, Samoa, or Poland.

Despite the 'cultural' diversity, the whole group got on quite well with each other. The tight-knit unit regularly socialised together in hotels (after work and on days off) and on weekend trips to Airlie Beach (78km south-east of Bowen) or one of the Whitsunday Islands.

On each working day, Irish-born Alec would bring his pet Staffordshire bull terrier to the tomato field. The friendly pooch would soon be adopted as the tomato-picking crew's mascot. Several years earlier, Alec had come across the abandoned pup on one of Bowen's beaches. The pup had originally been named Fred but he soon developed an uncanny skill for escaping from many locations (or situations). He was subsequently renamed, *Houdini.*

Each working morning, Alec would tie Houdini to a sturdy object such as a post, a tree, or a car axle. On numerous occasions, however, the clever pooch would still manage to find a way to escape, either by breaking the rope (or chain) or by squeezing his head through the leather collar around his neck.

With a newly-discovered sense of freedom, a *discreet* Houdini would casually stroll towards the tomato patch. Seeking some tender loving care, he would select the tomato-picker who was the furthest back in the tomato patch. Moving furtively between the rows, Houdini would sneakily place himself between his 'victim' and the bucket being filled with tomatoes. Rolling onto his back, he would demand a long pat and a belly rub.

Within a few minutes, most of the group had realised that Houdini had escaped. Alec, one of the faster tomato-pickers, would be working ahead of most of the others. Therefore, on most occasions, he would be one of the last people to know that Houdini had escaped!

Alec would then try to recapture Houdini. His efforts though were mostly futile; the mischievous pooch could be quite elusive. With assistance from several others, Houdini would be eventually caught and restrained. Next, Alec would escort the reluctant pooch (even having to carry him at times) back to where he had been previously chained or to a more secure location. If his vehicle was parked in a shady place, Alec would lock him inside. The windows would be wound down far enough for Houdini to poke his head through, but not far enough for him to climb out!

On one particular block of tomatoes, Houdini had previously befriended a crow. In a previous harvesting season, John Wayne had coined this particular block of tomatoes the *Wonder Patch*. He was quite dubious about the quality of tomatoes that would be produced on it. In past seasons, several types of diseases had affected the growth of the tomato bushes.

For the past five tomato-picking seasons, the crow would reacquaint itself with Houdini when the tomato-picking crew was toiling on this particular block of tomatoes. During the rest breaks, the itinerant workers would be entertained by what appeared to be some sort of communication between Houdini and the crow! In response to the cawing of the crow, the attention-seeking pooch would bark back – with crow-like noises.

During the two half-hour rest breaks, Alec would unleash Houdini and the affable pooch would casually wander around, greeting most (if not all) of the tomato-picking crew. The first person that Houdini sought out was one of the female tomato-pickers as she always had a large slice of Madeira cake for him!

Houdini's escapologist feats would soon earn him legendary status within the itinerant community (and in various locations across the three eastern states). One of his most notable feats of escape occurred one Saturday afternoon. Alec, along with Houdini, visited Dan (one of Charlie and Alec's co-workers) at his home. The two guys decided to venture to a nearby hotel for several hours, leaving Houdini in the 'secured' backyard of Dan's house. Alec wanted to chain Houdini to the clothesline but Dan was convinced that the pooch wouldn't be able to escape.

Several hours later, the pair returned to Dan's abode, and lo and behold, guess who was blissfully napping on the doormat *in front* of the house. Alec tried to be angry with Houdini but the affable pooch just simply rolled over onto his back, begging for a belly rub. Even worse, he appeared to be laughing' at Alec and Dan!

Alec led a self-satisfied Houdini back to the backyard and along with Dan, tried to figure out how Houdini managed to escape. They were half-expecting a hole to have been dug out under the fence. No hole had been dug but the garbage bin had been moved – next to the fence. A short time later, Dan's next-door neighbour emerged and with a wide grin on his face, explained to them how Houdini had escaped.

Just after Dan and Alec had left the house, Houdini knocked the garbage bin over and rolled it – with his head, towards the fence. Next, he pushed the bin into an upright position. Using it as a prop, Houdini got on top of the thick-paled wooden fence. After making his way along the fence, Houdini managed to climb onto a sturdy tree branch, near the top of the fence. From there, he made his way along another branch, which hovered above part of the roof of the house.

At this point, the next-door neighbour informed Dan that Houdini knew he was being watched. Undeterred, the mischievous pooch continued in his endeavour to escape. He casually strolled across the roof, until he came upon a tree in the front yard. He climbed down this tree and Houdini's afternoon adventure was just about to begin!

Dan and Alec would later learn that Houdini had wandered around the neighbourhood for quite a while. He eventually discovered the local butcher shop. Standing outside the building, with his face pressed against the window, Houdini began to whimper loudly and occasionally lick his lips. The butcher, at first, tried to ignore him but Houdini's persistence eventually earned him a large bone and several off-cuts! With a sense of accomplishment, Houdini slowly ambled back towards Dan's abode, settling down on the front door mat – waiting for Dan and Alec to return.

Away from the working environment, Charlie's social life continued to flourish, mainly in the Queens Beach area: located three kilometres north of Bowen's town centre. Many of his itinerant co-workers were regular patrons at the Queens Beach Hotel. Several of these co-workers had even decided to buy houses within the Bowen region, either staying in the area all year round or for most of the year. A notable exception, however, was a veteran itinerant worker named Gino, who had owned a house in Bowen for many years. Each year, he would work interstate for a period of five to seven months.

Gino was better known by his nickname 'Krusty'. His hairstyle was uncannily similar to a well-known character from the television show *The Simpsons*: Krusty the Clown. Krusty owned a four-bedroom house, a short distance from the town centre. During the tomato-picking season, he would rent out the three unused bedrooms. In his backyard, there were two medium-sized caravans, which were also rented out.

During each tomato-picking season, Krusty's house was a constant buzz of activity; dominated by frequent parties, at least several times per week. He rarely slept and often survived on extended power naps throughout the day – especially during workplace rest breaks. These frequent parties would eventually overwhelm some of the renters: victims of constant sleep deprivation. Subsequently, at least several renters every tomato-picking season would move out – seeking quieter accommodation.

Every Friday night, a large group of itinerant workers and nearby neighbours would either congregate inside Krusty's house or move to the more spacious backyard. Within the household, an abundance of activity would be in full swing. A constant flow of table tennis matches and Kelly pool competitions (played on a small billiards table) would be in full swing. In stark contrast, the main lounge area was far more sedate.

The room could be best described as a 'chill-out' area. Numerous illicit-substance deals would take place. Plastic bags of marijuana or 'chop-chop' (illegal tobacco) were exchanged for cash. Additionally, home-brewed alcohol was sampled and sold, albeit cheaply. As Krusty wouldn't allow any type of smoking within his house, the backyard was soon transformed into an aromatic and smoggy haven!

All the illicit substances being sold had been grown in several different regions (across four states) of Australia: in southern rural regions of Queensland; the Central Tablelands area in NSW; the southern highlands of NSW; several rural regions of South Australia; and, in south-eastern Victoria (especially the chop-chop). On several occasions, before the commencement of the tomato-picking season, Charlie would transport large amounts of chop-chop from northern Victorian (which had been grown in the south-east of Victoria) to Bowen. In return, his *entire* fuel costs would be paid by the recipient.

Charlie soon learnt that most of the dealing in illicit substances would either take place in residential premises, caravan parks, or during rest breaks on tomato farms. Illicit substance transactions rarely took place in the hotels – there was a good reason for this. The itinerant community was well aware of *Drug Squad* officers working undercover as bar staff or as 'regular' patrons! Veteran itinerants, in particular, tended to quickly 'suss out' these individuals. Generally, they did not fit into the itinerant social culture and the three key tell-tale signs were:

1. Lingering around certain hotels trying to be 'friendly' towards certain itinerant workers.
2. Still loitering around in hotels after two weeks and noticeably not engaged in any form of employment.
3. The bar staff was 'inquisitive' or 'over–observant'.

The only people who would stay in the Bowen region for more than two weeks at a time were either working itinerants/backpackers or interstate retirees. The retirees (mostly aged 50+) tended to frequent establishments such as the RSL Club, the Yachting Club, or the Golf Club. Itinerant/backpacker patronage at these three venues was generally quite minimal.

Meanwhile, on the tomato farm, the atmosphere between John Wayne and the itinerant workers was mostly one of a positive and harmonious nature. However, there was a notable 'thorn' within the group – Rhoda: the tomato field boss. Standing at 1.80 metres tall and of a large body frame, she was quite an imposing figure.

Originally, Rhoda attempted to obtain employment in the tomato packing shed but John was seeking a paddock boss to keep the tomato-picking crew 'inline'. During the working day, she would regularly walk (slowly) up and down the rows of the tomato block, occasionally doing bucket checks. In an attempt to be authoritative, Rhoda would raise her shoulders and bellow (with an oft-reddened face) at the hapless tomato-picker if she found more than the *allowable* defective tomatoes in their bucket.

The itinerant workers, however, soon discovered a major chink in Rhoda's armour. She easily succumbed to most forms of humour. Charlie, for example, was regularly hung-over or in a state of 'seediness' (feeling unwell or queasy) within the first couple of hours of the working day. Therefore, his level of concentration tended to be well below the required level!

So, when Rhoda berated him for having too many defective (or over-ripe) tomatoes in his buckets, Charlie would casually inform her that the brightness of the sun affected his ability to tell the difference between a green tomato and a red one! In response, Rhoda would chuckle loudly and at times, uncontrollably. Any issue concerning defective tomatoes quickly dissipated. Other tomato-pickers were also equally 'imaginative' in their response to any unfavourable bucket check!

Rhoda's dress sense was practically the same every day: a large well-worn Akubra hat; a sweat-stained khaki shirt; tight-fitting khaki bicycle pants; black cowgirl boots; dark sunglasses; and, an excessive amount of bright pink lipstick. A fan of Rockabilly music, one of the itinerant collective soon had a nickname for her: *Rockin Rhoda.*

Several of the female tomato pickers who regularly clashed with Rhoda, however, cruelly gave her another nickname: *Silverback.* One of these female pickers described Rhoda's upper-body movements as akin to a silverback gorilla – chest puffed out, shoulders raised, and with her arms seemingly dangled loosely whilst she slowly walked. Despite the occasional clashes, the majority of the tomato-picking crew liked Rhoda and thus, got on quite well with her. They regularly tried to get her to socialise with them but Rhoda was mostly contented to just chill out at home outside work hours.

At the end of the tomato-picking season, John Wayne organised an end-of-season get-together for all of his employees (tomato pickers, packing shed workers, farmhands, etc) in a function room of the Queens Beach Hotel. He paid for all of the food and all beverages, except for spirit drinks. With plenty of coaxing from many of the tomato-pickers, Rhoda also attended. A 'gastronomic' over-indulgence and 'social inebriation' were enjoyed by all and sundry that night.

An enjoyable and highly profitable tomato-picking season had come to an end. Charlie was soon driving along the Bruce Highway again, in a southerly direction towards the city of Brisbane. After staying in the cities of Brisbane and the Gold Coast for a week, he recommenced his journey, driving towards the town of Young (in the South West Slopes region of New South Wales). Another cherry-picking season was about to begin.

12

The Wombat Tales

Charlie arrived in Young in the mid-afternoon and instantly made a beeline to one of the town's hotels. Inside the Patriot Hotel and with a schooner of beer in his hand, he was soon discussing with several itinerants (who he had worked with during the recent Bowen tomato-picking season) the upcoming cherry-picking season in the region.

This particular group of itinerant workers had already commenced employment on an orchard, located 13km southwest of Young. Charlie was informed that there were no employment opportunities for him at this particular orchard. Instead, he was given handwritten directions to another nearby orchard: Zadonich and Sons Cherry Orchard.

An hour and a half later, Charlie was driving along the Olympic Highway, heading towards the small town of Wombat (15km southwest of Young). After travelling a distance of about 12 kilometres, he came upon a roadside fruit shop. Perched on top of the front awning was a large sign: 'Cherries for Sale'. Charlie entered the shop.

After being directed to drive along the unsealed laneway that started from the fruit shop (and perpendicular to the

Olympic Highway), Charlie soon came upon a medium-sized packing shed. A few minutes later, he was engaged in a light-hearted conversation with Bernie Zadonich, the orchard owner. Charlie was soon directed to the nearby camping area, which contained a large amenities block and numerous powered sites. Better still, he could commence employment the next day.

As Charlie was pitching his tent, fellow cherry-pickers were returning to the campsite. The campsite comprised of a mixture of tents, caravans, campervans, and even refurbished buses. In a corner of the camping ground, stood a small (but neatly restored) hut that looked like it was probably constructed decades ago.

After Charlie had finished erecting his large four-person tent, an elderly Aboriginal gentleman emerged from the hut and approached him. Greeting Charlie with a broad friendly smile, he introduced himself as Elwood. Over the next few weeks, the pair would regularly converse. Charlie instantly took a liking to him, deeming him a delightful character.

Elwood had lived in the small hut for more than twenty-five years. Although he resided in the quaint-sized abode for a good part of the year, Elwood often travelled throughout the rural areas of New South Wales and Victoria, performing as a 'Country and Western' musical artist.

In the evenings, after a hard day's toil of cherry-picking, Elwood would relax in an antiquated cane-woven chair near the doorway of the hut. Wearing a dark grey Akubra hat, he began playing his acoustic guitar and sang softly to himself, reminiscing some of his favourite country music songs. During the fruit-picking seasons, Elwood would perform in a hotel or an Ex-Services/RSL club on weekends, either in Young or nearby towns. Over the next few weeks, Charlie would notice that the Akubra rarely left Elwood's head!

As Charlie had encountered previously on many occasions, the campsite 'commune' contained a vast array of intriguing characters. Firstly, there was Hank and Tammy: a couple aged in their sixties. Like Elwood, they were ardent fans of country music. Each day, they would bring their 'ghetto blaster' to the orchard. Old-styled country and western music (e.g. Slim Dusty, Hank Williams Snr, George Jones, Willie Nelson, etc.) would calmly bellow throughout the cherry orchard block.

Hank and Tammy, also, wore large Akubra hats – practically all the time. Charlie began to wonder if they ever removed them – even whilst showering or sleeping. The couple had known Elwood for a long time. Over the years, they had followed him on numerous occasions to watch him perform professionally in various rural towns and cities.

By the end of the first week, Charlie had learnt a significant fact; nearly half of the campsite residents were *related* to each other. The majority of them came from the nearby towns of Harden, Temora, and Cootamundra. Some of the group even belonged to one family, spread over four generations. The matriarch of this clan was Joyce, an elderly widow.

Joyce dwelled in a small caravan next to Charlie's tent. A friendly lady, she would converse with Charlie daily, mainly outside work hours though. She proudly declared to him that she had had eleven children and a countless number of grandchildren (along with several great-grandchildren, as well). Joyce further added that a few of her 'kids' and grandchildren had been making the annual pilgrimage to the Wombat region for the cherry-picking season (and stone fruit picking season) for many years. Charlie would also soon learn that Joyce had quite a *colourful* history.

Although Joyce spoke fluent English, she did so with a distinct and unusual accent. Eventually, Charlie queried her about this acquired accent. Somewhat reluctantly, Joyce stated that she was born in Russia but her family had moved to Germany in her early teens. She also informed Charlie that her actual Christian name was Lilliana.

Initially, Charlie thought that Joyce was aged in her early seventies but Elwood informed him that she was 84 years old! Joyce's mass of thick black hair (dyed and permed) did make her appear younger though. Whilst picking cherries, Joyce would wear what looked like an old air-force cap. One day, an intrigued Charlie gently enquired about the history of this cap. She stated to Charlie that the cap had belonged to her deceased husband who had passed away two decades ago. He was a former air force pilot. The dark blue cap was, surprisingly, still in a good condition – obviously, well looked after by Joyce.

Joyce was *always* dressed in old-style floral dresses that went well past her knees, even whilst she picked cherries. In the morning, she would wear a dark blue cardigan, but it soon came off as the day quickly warmed.

With the well-worn air force cap, long floral dress, cardigan, and fashionable laced-up black boots, Joyce certainly stood out from the other cherry pickers! The majority of the workers, especially the itinerants, wore standard trousers/tracksuit pants with long-sleeved thin cotton shirts.

Orchard management ensured that Joyce would only be picking cherries on trees that didn't require any (or limited) ladder work. Most of the ladders used in this orchard had six rungs. Joyce, on the other hand, had the use of the lone platform step ladder, which consisted of only three steps.

Although Joyce picked cherries at a relatively slow rate, she would still work consistently throughout the day – and, for at least eight hours. Her daily tally of full lugs (rectangular-shaped plastic baskets) of cherries even surpassed the efforts of the younger members of her clan on many occasions! The orchard owner, Bernie, and two of Joyce's sons (Ted and Neville) would regularly remind several of the lazy youngsters of this feat; mostly in a light-hearted manner though.

Ted, a veteran itinerant fruit-picker, was one of the fastest cherry-pickers on the orchard – and was also a great storyteller. Charlie soon learnt that he had a long-standing reputation for creating fantasised/fabricated accounts of past events. Or in other words – distorting the truth. His overall persona reminded Charlie of a well-known Australian television character: Ted Bullpit from the TV series *Kingswood Country*. He (Charlie) soon had a nickname for him – 'Ted Bullshit'.

Neville (Ted's brother), on the other hand, was quite a subdued character. Along with his wife, Sharon, their conversational skills seemed to be quite minimal. The pair sported numerous tattoos, had missing or damaged teeth, and easy-visible facial scarring. Charlie deemed them as a pair of *hard nuts* and, at times, found it difficult to initiate any sort of discussion with them. Halfway through the cherry-picking season, Charlie discovered that Neville had only been released from jail three months prior. He had served a few years for armed robbery.

Life in the orchard, especially outside work hours, could be quite mundane at times for the campsite residents. Thus, in an attempt to alleviate this boredom, many of them (including Charlie) would either venture to the city of Young or the Wombat Hotel (5 kilometres from the orchard) several times per week. The expeditions to Young often comprised of the following sequence: hotel/club patronage; grocery shopping; and, a takeaway meal from Young's lone Chinese Restaurant: *Wok and Roll.*

The Wombat Hotel had quite an interesting history. A pivotal part of a former gold mining area, the hotel has the distinction of having the longest continuous liquor licence in the state of New South Wales – since 1877. Over the past few decades, the Wombat Hotel had been a popular meeting place for itinerant fruit pickers, orchard hands, and orchardists/farmers who resided within the Harden Shire. The hotel is situated just off the Olympic Highway, nestled within the small town of Wombat. This historical hotel establishment was also well known for its damper burgers!

These huge burgers comprised of several beef patties, bacon, eggs, beetroot, pineapple, coleslaw, cheese, tomato, and lettuce – all heaped between two large slices of homemade damper bread and were three to four times the size of a normal hamburger bun. It was also known as the *heart-attack* burger.

As the vast majority of people could not eat all of this culinary delight, the oversized damper burger had soon gained legendary status within the local and itinerant communities. The ability of an individual to devour this *gluttonous* item (without the aid of digestive fluids, such as beer) earned them substantial bragging rights.

The then-owners, Ron and Sheree, had owned the Wombat Hotel for the past several years.

As with many traditional hotel establishments owned by a couple, Ron was in charge of the bar whilst Sheree was in charge of the kitchen. As the 'Damper Burger Challenge' had been a popular tradition over previous years, they were quite happy to continue this novelty pastime. Ron had even attached a sizeable whiteboard to the wall behind the bar, listing the names of all the successful *damper burger conquerors* (along with the date of conquest written beside their name)!

On most nights, the Wombat Hotel was a hub of boisterous activity. Fuelled by a substantial intake of alcohol, some patrons could be quite animated – and aggressive. Inevitably, this kind of behaviour often led to minor bouts of pugilism. Fortunately, most fracases were swiftly quelled and peace within the licenced establishment was once more restored. Then one Friday night!

What began as a one-on-one 'pugilistic disagreement' soon erupted into a more volatile situation. Several tables and chairs were either upended or knocked down; glasses of beer were spilled or knocked over. At first, Ron and several regular patrons were unable to quell the melee as it had involved quite a few people. The melee was made worse by Carl (an itinerant worker), one of the two instigators, who deliberately escalated the situation by punching several people at random and knocking drinks off tables with his arms. Without warning, Sheree suddenly emerged with a baseball bat and struck Carl's legs several times. Her actions had the desired effect and he collapsed to the ground in agony. The melee, in turn, came to an abrupt halt!

Similar incidents in the hotel were always dealt with by the owner/licensee and with assistance from other patrons. Police were never called as the nearest police station (in Young) was fifteen kilometres away. Carl was banned for life from entering the Wombat Hotel again. Two days later, his employment in one of the local orchards was terminated. The consensus within the area was that Carl needed to be *run out of town.*

On Zadonich's orchard, the general atmosphere was mostly one of a calm and peaceful nature – until one late Saturday night. Two of Elwood's grand-nephews, Jake and Cab, had been staying in the hut the past two days. Sitting on chairs outside the hut, the pair had initially been quite civil towards each other. As the intake of alcohol steadily increased, however, the mood between them soon soured. There had been 'bad blood' between them in the past. An intoxicated Cab started teasing Jake about his past failed encounters with women!

Elwood tried to calm the situation but to no avail. Jake and Cab's raucous behaviour soon alerted some of the campsite residents. To assist Elwood, they ventured towards the hut. Jake then punched Cab, connecting with his jaw who, subsequently, dropped to the ground – knocked out cold. Whilst he was being restrained by several of the residents, a normally-calm Elwood delivered an angry tirade – centimetres from Jake's face. Jake quietly retreated, dropping his head despondently, and was led back into the hut.

Whilst it was suggested to Elwood that Cab should be taken to the casualty ward of the Young Hospital, he was steadfast against the idea. Elwood didn't want to attract police attention. Angrily flustered, he further added that Cab had actually been the instigator of the fracas and probably got what he deserved.

Early the next morning, Elwood awoke both of his troublesome grand-nephews and quite audibly, gave them a stern lecture about their inappropriate behaviour towards each other. Upon hearing the audible tirade, Charlie poked his head out of his tent. Elwood was also gesticulating wildly in front of both Jake and Cab, who was now outside the hut. Two hours later, the pair drove away from the campsite – together. Elwood, feeling much calmer by now, casually made his way to the orchard for another day's cherry-picking.

After six weeks, the cherry-picking season in the Wombat area came to a close. Charlie had managed to save quite a substantial amount of his overall earnings. It was at this point that Charlie decided to plan his first overseas venture: a mixture of working and travelling. Six months later, this idea would come to fruition.

Charlie had planned to move to the Orange (NSW) region for the remainder of their cherry-picking season. Via the itinerant fruit-picker 'network', however, he learned that unfavourable weather conditions had already caused substantial damage to their overall cherry harvest. Charlie was further informed that the upcoming cherry-picking season in the Shepparton (Victoria) region would be a better option economically. Before departing from Zadonich's orchard, he managed to secure employment in a large orchard, situated near the small town of Ratatutra (20 kilometres from the city of Shepparton).

13

From Dairyland to Wanderlust
Countdown

On a glorious summer's day in early December, Charlie drove into Dairyland Orchards, located a few kilometres from the town of Ratatutra. After driving along a narrow well-tarred laneway, he parked his vehicle in the designated visitors' car park. Charlie entered the packing shed. The modern-designed complex was quite spectacular and purposefully well-organised and it was huge; complete with expensive-looking and immaculately clean state-of-the-art machinery.

After walking up the wooden stylishly-designed staircase, Charlie entered the office where he was immediately greeted by a friendly, but over-enthusiastic administrative receptionist. A few minutes later, she introduced him to the company's managing director (Hubert) just as he entered the office. In stark contrast, Hubert was quite a passive character.

Hubert stated that the cherry-picking season would commence in about three or four days. Then, he directed Charlie to the spacious accommodation area, about fifty metres away from the packing shed. Two red-bricked buildings dominated this area. Both buildings contained single-room accommodation (colloquially known as 'huts') and a large kitchen. Additionally, one of these buildings contained a spacious lounge area and a large cool room (for refrigerating groceries). Both kitchens contained several freezers.

As all the rooms were already occupied, Charlie erected his large tent on a powered camping site. The powered sites were occupied by both caravan dwellers and tent dwellers. He pitched his tent between a small tent and one of the caravans. The accommodation area was largely deserted as most of the itinerant workers were either engaged in menial orchard work or patronising one of Ratatutra's three hotels.

By the late evening, Charlie would meet some of the itinerants/backpackers. Once again, he would encounter a diverse range of personalities, commencing with Sven. Swedish-born Sven was a New Zealand citizen aged in his mid-fifties who had spent a considerable portion of his life globe-hopping. Gentle-natured Sven was quite a conversationalist and seemed to relish any opportunity to share his past travelling adventures.

As Charlie had already commenced the planning phase of his near-future overseas venture, he would be one of Sven's more receptive listeners. Throughout the upcoming cherry-picking season, Charlie would discuss with him, on a near-daily basis, wanderlust-related topics. Aside from imparting his past travelling experiences, Sven had two other notable interests: punting on racehorses and astronomy. Sven's punting ability would be more profitable than his fruit-picking capabilities! He largely regarded fruit-picking employment as 'paid outdoor exercise'.

An avid amateur astronomer, Sven was also a member of several astronomy groups. On any calm and cloud-free night (where the stars and the moon were visible), he would position his telescope (perched on a high stand) just outside the accommodation perimeter – even in the early-morning hours at times.

Charlie, along with several others, would join Sven outside. Each individual would take turns gazing through the highly magnified eyepiece at a particular star or certain landmarks on the surface of the moon. In a nerdy-like fashion, Sven would deliver an in-depth explanation, describing what the person was actually viewing!

Many of the younger itinerants regarded Sven as a little bit weird. In turn, he didn't particularly like them either! Sven strongly detested the smell of marijuana – and loud noises. One night, Sven retired to bed relatively early. Several of the hut dwellers decided to have a 'Bong and Beer' party in the lounge room of the first accommodation building – next-door to Sven's room. As the intake of mind-altering substances increased, so did the volume of the music being played on a stereo system. Despite being a reasonable distance away, the loud music even awoke Charlie several times in the wee hours of the morning.

Just after 5.30 am, an irate Sven emerged from his hut (room). As soon as he entered the lounge room, Sven turned on the television, *loudly*. Next, he went back to his room and turned on his transistor radio, *loudly*. Once he had finished drinking his cup of coffee, Sven decided to walk up and down between the two buildings, hitting a pan and a pot against each other for several minutes. Fortunately, Charlie and several other residents were already awake. However, they all decided to use the kitchen in the other red-bricked building complex!

Two of the late-night offenders sheepishly entered the second kitchen. One of them sarcastically moaned, 'I didn't know that loud noises existed this early in the morning!'

Charlie immediately responded, 'Well, it's not a bright idea to upset Sven… especially when he is trying to have a good night's sleep!'

Aforementioned, Sven practically treated the itinerant fruit-picking lifestyle as a form of paid outdoor exercise. Although he had been part of the itinerant fruit-picking circuit for more than ten years, Sven was quite content to toil at a leisurely pace. Volly (whose actual first name was Valdek), the cherry-orchard supervisor, regularly tried to 'encourage' him to pick the cherries at a faster rate but to no avail.

Sven would often irk Volly as he was notorious for leaving cherries on the top sections of the row of trees. A bellowing Volly would then order him to scale his ladder and remove all the missed cherries, before moving on to the next row of cherries.

A person not removing all the cherries from the tops of the trees was Volly's number one pet hate. A common practice, in the late afternoon, involved an individual who would finish filling their last lug of cherries for the day, deliberately leaving cherries on top of the trees. As Volly wanted the block of cherry trees to be properly picked, before moving on to the next block, he would seek *volunteers.*

Oddly enough, the larger cherries (and often in sizeable clusters) tended to be in the top section of the cherry tree. Charlie would gleefully volunteer and, despite having to go up and down a ladder, quickly discovered that he could fill a cherry lug at a faster rate. As a bonus, a grateful Volly would ensure that the volunteers, in upcoming days, would be allocated the 'better' rows of cherry trees to pick.

Although Volly could be quite a hostile character at times, he was a good people-organiser though. Regularly riding his quad bike in between the rows of cherry trees at a 'hair-raising' speed, Volly never crashed into anything – or anyone. His volatile nature often resulted in disagreements with many of the cherry pickers. Some of the veteran itinerant workers would sometimes refer to him as 'Volly Vanker' – even right in front of his face.

Each day, there would be between 80-100 cherry pickers in a block of cherries. Therefore, during the working day, a large number of filled lugs needed to be picked up and transported back to the shed. Several gentlemen, all aged in their 60s, were employed to carry out this task. Collectively, they became known as *Dad's Army*.

They would drive up and down between the rows of cherries on small grey 'Fergie' tractors, each towing a small wooden dray. They would lift the full lugs of cherries and place them onto the dray, once Volly (using a hole-puncher) had punched the cherry-picker's tally card. At the end of each working day, Volly would collect all these tally cards and hand them into the orchard office.

The chief stalwart of the group was Jim, who was better known as 'Jammy'. For more than a decade, he had been living in a caravan in the orchard's accommodation area. During the working day, Jammy was mainly a pleasant and friendly chap. Outside work hours, however, he was notoriously known for transforming into a *Dr. Jekyll and Mr. Hyde* character. This was largely due to his regular and excessive intake of alcohol.

Over the years, Jammy had been barred from the three hotels in Ratatutra and several other hotels (in nearby small towns) on numerous occasions. Despite approaching the age of seventy, he could still be quite feisty with other hotel patrons!

Although Jammy was usually the instigator, he would rarely be engaged in any pugilistic activity. On many occasions, Jammy would raise his fists in an attempt to provoke his adversary, but his age and slightly-built stature generally ensured that he would not be harmed. At that point, publicans and hotel staff would refuse to serve him any more alcohol and they would also arrange a local taxi to take him back to the orchard – escorting or forcibly assisting him to the vehicle if necessary.

During the second week of the cherry-picking season, Charlie was awoken late one night by a loud commotion nearby. After emerging from his tent, he could hear a barrage of barely-intelligible swear words coming from within Jammy's caravan, along with numerous items being hurled against its walls.

Fearing that he may be involved in a physical altercation, Charlie and several others (Todd, Ronald, and Rob) rushed to his caravan. Todd instantly opened the caravan door and the potential rescuers were immediately overwhelmed by the strong smell of alcohol. Jammy, in a drunken rage, had been arguing with himself and trashing the inside of his caravan!

Todd just glared at him and bellowed, 'Jammy … shut the fuck up!'

He instantly retreated and laid down on his dishevelled bed. About fifteen seconds later, Jammy was snoring (and snorting) the night away!

Todd, a former miner, had worked in several mines in the states of Queensland and Western Australia. During those mining years, he had used his substantial earnings to purchase two houses: both of them in the Sunshine Coast (Queensland) region. Upon retiring from mining, Todd decided to join the 'Harvest Trail' as a means of travelling around Australia.

Ronald was from a region in far north Queensland. Travelling south a distance of over 2400 kilometres, it was the first time in his life that he travelled outside his local area. Whilst he would be deemed as a gentle-natured character, it soon emerged that he was a relatively poor conversationalist. When anyone attempted to initiate any fruitful conversation with him, he would somehow link it to his employment history, which largely revolved around the use of farming equipment. Especially tractors and combine harvesters.

Ronald's sheltered-life level of conversational skills soon irked some of the itinerant workers. Todd in particular. Although Todd's general persona could be best described as being boorish or uncultivated, he could still easily converse with others on a wide range of topics. Ronald's limited conversational skills soon earned him the name 'tractor boy' (coined by Todd). Tactless Todd even went a step further, occasionally greeting him in the morning with the line: 'Good morning … *tractor boy.*'

Then there was Rob, a veteran itinerant worker aged in his mid-fifties, who had been 'on the road' in Australia and New Zealand for several decades. An extroverted character, he would discuss (incessantly at times) his previous travels and adventures, largely in the form of an implausible yarn. After listening to one of Rob's lengthy riveting tales one night, Charlie turned to Todd and sarcastically quipped, 'Perhaps Rob should consider a career as a children's author… he's a great storyteller!'

On one particular evening, a group of campsite residents (mainly young backpackers) had gathered together around a large kitchen table. Displaying a façade of awe and wonderment, they patiently listened to yet another one of Rob's exhilarating tales of past travel escapades. Eventually, he paused (to take a breath) and Todd instantly remarked, 'Hey Rob, with all the things that you have done … you must be at least two hundred years old by now!'

A now-disheartened Rob went uncharacteristically quiet. Charlie (over muffled laughter) soon assured him that the audience was enjoying his epic tales of past adventure and urged him to continue. Moments later, a rejuvenated and animated Rob was once more babbling away!

The captive audience was from several foreign countries: New Zealand, Japan, the United Kingdom, Netherlands, Denmark, and Belgium. Except for Hal, who was originally from Sydney.

Hal, aged in his mid-thirties, had spent the past two decades either as an itinerant fruit-picker or as an inmate in several different prisons (and juvenile detention centres) across several Australian states. His erratic persona at times soon earned him the nickname 'Psycho' (courtesy of Todd again). On the right side of Hal's face, a distinct ten-centimetre scar overshadowed numerous minor ones. When Todd queried him about the origin of this distinctive scar, Hal declared that he had been slashed in the face with broken glass in a past hotel skirmish.

Hal further admitted to Charlie and Todd that he had a *long* history of bar-room brawling, along with being involved in several unsavoury incidents whilst spending time within the prison system. Two years later, Hal was involved in a vicious skirmish in one of Ratatutra's hotels. He was charged with several offences and, subsequently, received another prison sentence

The group of young backpackers was an intriguing lot – the males especially. These young males tended to spend a considerable amount of their daily time 'wooing' the young females! Even in the orchard, attempts of courtship were quite evident as the young backpackers generally tended to work near each other. Towards the end of each working day, the young lads would often help the young lasses fill their last lugs of cherries!

In the accommodation area, they tended to congregate in the second kitchen. All of them were either dwelling in tents or small vans/campervans, close to each other. The caravan dwellers, the veteran itinerants, were on the right side of Charlie's tent. The backpackers dwelt on the left side (of Charlie's tent).

Tim, one of the English backpackers, had been venturing within Australia in a relatively old 'beat-up' van. Although there was a double-sized mattress inside the van, Tim mainly slept in a small tent, pitched next to his vehicle. During the cherry-picking season, his van would become known as the 'shagmobile' as it would be used for sexual liaisons, mainly within the backpacker community, from time to time. In the last two weeks of the cherry-picking season, however, Tim would use his van regularly. He had become 'romantically' linked with *two* of the young female backpackers.

Next-door to Charlie's tent was a small tent, occupied by a Belgian woman. Sabina, who was aged in her mid-twenties, only occasionally socialised with the other young backpackers. She would never become 'romantically' linked with any of the young backpacker males. On most afternoons and occasionally in the evenings as well, Sabina could be seen conversing with Charlie. They both sat on a patch of grass in front of their respective tents.

One evening, as they conversed over several glasses of vodka and orange juice, Charlie plucked up the courage to convey his feelings for her. Sabina, playfully, grabbed his shirt collar and led him back to the inside of his tent! On a comfortable double-sized mattress, a session of intense passion soon followed and she stayed with him the entire night.

Meanwhile, life in the cherry orchard itself was seldom dull, largely due to the constant buzz of activity. Various sound systems regularly blared throughout the orchard. To quell the daily mundane process of cherry-picking, an aura of daily competitiveness soon became prevalent amongst many of the cherry-pickers. The constant roar of tractors and quad bikes ensured any lack of tranquillity throughout the working day. Additionally, the ever-present booming voice of Volly could be heard regularly throughout the orchard each working day.

An obnoxious Volly regularly 'roared' (but mostly in jest) at the cherry-pickers. Certain cherry-pickers, however, did irk him from time to time; especially doing a 'poor job'. Doing a *poor job* included the following: picking too many cherries without stems; not filling the cherry lugs up to the required level; and, filling the lugs with too much foliage (an excess amount of leaves, tree twigs, and buds/spurs). Two of the worst offenders were one particular couple: Carla and Bongo (no one knew his actual Christian name). Volly would often clash with them – especially with Carla.

Working together, the couple would consistently pick a high tally of lugs (of cherries) each day. Volly and the 'Dad's Army brigade" would regularly check the quality of their full lugs of cherries and they would constantly discover a large amount of foliage (especially buds) and an unacceptable percentage of stemless cherries. Volly would then try to belittle and embarrass the pair but to no avail.

Whilst Bongo was a mostly subdued character, Carla, on the other hand, could be quite antagonistic towards Volly. Gravelly voiced, deeply tanned (but with weather-beaten skin), and skimpily dressed she would regularly flirt with Volly and the Dad's Army collective (especially Jammy) – and Hubert.

During the cherry-picking season, several itinerant workers had their employment services terminated for not doing the job properly. Hubert was most likely the reason why Carla and Bongo were not dismissed. Rumours soon emerged that Hubert and Carla were on *very friendly* terms. Carla would also earn the ire of most of the itinerant collective. Initially, Charlie and Todd thought that the well-travelled Carla was aged in her late forties. They were quite shocked to discover that Carla was only in her early thirties!

Bongo reminded Charlie of a certain television character from a bygone decade, namely Catweazle. *Catweazle* was a television series that screened between 1970 and 1971. Similar in appearance to Catweazle, Bongo sported long mangy and mostly-unwashed hair, along with a lengthy and straggly (and greying) goatee beard. Aged in his mid-forties, he was not deemed as being problematic (like Carla) and, subsequently, most of the itinerant community would converse amicably with him. In stark contrast, Carla's overall behavior, along with her loud gravelly emphysemic-sounding voice irked all and sundry.

Before commencing a relationship with Bongo, Carla had spent the past decade working as a jillaroo in the outback regions of Queensland and the Northern Territory. According to Jammy and Volly, she was a heavy drinker and smoker (both cigarettes and marijuana). They further stated to the itinerant collective that both Carla and Bongo had built up sizeable criminal records over many years, mainly for possession and supply of illegal substances. Two years later, Charlie (whilst working in North Queensland) learnt that Carla was serving time in a Victorian jail after being charged with several drug offences and a botched attempt to burn her car as a means of collecting insurance money!

Two days after Christmas Day, the cherry-picking season came to a halt. Three days later, Charlie found further employment in an orchard in the Ardmona region (15 kilometres from the town of Ratatutra) picking apricots. This type of employment would only last for two weeks. As there was no accommodation available in this particular orchard, Charlie stayed at the nearby Jumanji Hotel.

Whilst some orchards would select-pick the apricots on several separate occasions, this orchard would only select-pick twice. The first select-picking mainly involved using a ladder, removing the ripened fruit from the tops of the trees and the 'tips' (the ends) of the branches. The rest of the apricots were removed from the tree a few days later.

On this particular orchard, all the apricot pickers were paid in cash (placed in an envelope). In future years, Charlie would gain employment in this orchard during the apricot-picking season on several occasions. Eventually, a housing estate (which had been building up over several years) had reached the boundary of the orchard. At this point, the elderly orchardist and one of his sons decided to raze the orchard – removing all the fruit trees. This was achieved via the use of a bulldozer and a groundbreaker (also known as a land leveller). They then sold the cleared land, subdividing it for housing construction; a decision that would prove to be far more profitable than orcharding!

Once the apricot-picking season had ceased, Charlie was back on the road once more, driving along the Hume Freeway towards Sydney. During his short stay in Sydney, he purchased a one-way flight ticket to London (United

Kingdom). Charlie's departure date would be on the 29th of May.

After leaving Sydney, Charlie drove in a westerly direction along the Great Western Highway. After driving through the city of Bathurst, he continued his journey along the Mitchell Highway. Charlie ended the three-hour road journey in the small town of Lucknow (10 kilometres from the city of Orange). After several beers at the lone tavern, he was back in Kevin and Alan's orchard once again. The next three and a half months would be a solid period of employment for Charlie. His main goal: save as much money as he could for his overseas wanderlust adventure.

Life for Charlie, during this particular fruit-picking season, was quite routine and, thus, mundane. In late April, though, a major incident occurred in sleepy Lucknow. One late morning, the driver of a semi-trailer truck lost control of his vehicle after swerving to miss a car that had carelessly turned in front of him. The large rig crashed into the sidewall of the tavern. No one was in the lounge section of the tavern at the time. Norm, the owner-publican, was the only person inside the tavern at the time. Fortunately, he was well away from the lounge area.

Later that afternoon, Charlie was discussing the incident with Jed and Spud outside the damaged tavern. Nearby, Norm was discussing the situation with a police officer and two insurance company representatives. Strangely though, he was noticeably cheerful – practically grinning from ear to ear. Spud declared to Charlie that this was the first time that he had ever seen Norm smile!

Several months later, Norm sold the tavern after reaping the benefits of using the insurance money to refurbish the establishment. He left the local area shortly afterward, never to be heard of again.

In a further endeavour to boost his level of savings, Charlie sold his beloved *Tank* several days after the completion of the fruit-picking season. The following morning, he was aboard an XPT locomotive, bound for Sydney's Central Railway Station. Two days later, Charlie was on a one-way flight to London.

About the Author

P.J. Kropp was born in rural New South Wales (Australia) in 1965.

After completing a Diploma in Education (high school teaching) in Sydney in 1987, P.J. Kropp decided not to enter the teaching profession the following year. Instead, he returned to his home city (Orange) in December 1987 and commenced employment (fruit picking) in one of the local orchards.

In mid-2008, P.J. Kropp decided to farewell the itinerant lifestyle, relocating to the Victorian state capital: Melbourne. At the age of 43, and after an absence of 21 years, he was a full-time student once more! P.J. Kropp completed a Bachelor's Degree in IT (Business Information Systems) in 2014.

It all began in early-January 1988 when P.J. Kropp left Orange and travelled to Griffith (NSW) to work in a vineyard and, a short time later, onto Cobram (Victoria) for the pear-picking season. By mid-February, he was back in Orange for the fruit-picking season (pears, stone fruits, and apples). Whilst in Orange, P.J.Kropp decided to adopt an itinerant lifestyle, via fruit-picking throughout the three eastern states of Australia. Over the next twenty years, he would persevere with this largely unconventional lifestyle: a lifestyle that would also take him beyond the Australian shores, from time to time.

This is the first book of a two-book series (the second book to be published at the end of next year or early-2021). In the early 1990s, P.J. Kropp began to jot down handwritten notes as he constantly travelled throughout the eastern states of Australia and abroad (several European countries and New Zealand, in particular).

Originally, P.J. Kropp tackled both literary projects as autobiographical accounts. However, he soon realised that a different approach was required: a fictional-based one. Although, most of the content of this book is largely fictional, everything is based on actual events and real people!